# Wyoming Double-Cross

When the notorious Blair Wilton and his gang of outlaws decide to raid the bank at Medicine Bow, they send in Chicago confidence trickster Paul Springer to reconnoitre the town. Here a chance encounter with an old acquaintance from the windy city causes Springer to change his plans suddenly.

To add to the outlaws' woes, Jack Stone, the famous Kentuckian gunfighter, enters into the fray and goes up against Wilton and his gang.

Will it be Stone or Wilton who survives the final, deadly confrontation?

Corrigan's Revenge
The Fourth of July
Showdown at Medicine Creek
The Sheriff of Fletcher County
Coyote Winter
Judgement at Red Rock
The Man Who Tamed Mallory
Ghost Town
The Smiling Gunman
The Marshal from Hell
The Legend of Injun Joe Brady
The Wolf River Outfit
A Hero of the West
Massacre in Moose City
Lattegan's Loot
Incident at Mustang Pass
Sharkey's Raiders
The Coyotero Kid
The Devil's Left Hand
Christmas at Horseshoe Bend
Portrait of an Outlaw
The Vengeance Trail

# Wyoming Double-Cross

J.D. Kincaid

A Black Horse Western

ROBERT HALE · LONDON

ISBN 978-0-7090-9168-4

Robert Hale Limited
Clerkenwell House
Clerkenwell Green
London EC1R 0HT

www.halebooks.com

Typeset by
Derek Doyle & Associates, Shaw Heath
Printed and bound in Great Britain by
CPI Antony Rowe, Chippenham and Eastbourne

# APRIL 1879

# ONE

Kid Sawyer trotted along the north-western bank of the Colorado River towards the small township of Rifle. His black mare was bone-weary and flagging. So was the Kid. He had been hired as a ranch-hand-cum-gunman in the range war that had recently taken place in Lincoln County, New Mexico. He had entered the fray as a brash yet naïve youngster, adept with both a six-gun and a rifle and eagerly looking for adventure. As the war progressed, however, the killing sickened him and, although he now had a reputation as a fearsome and ruthless gunslinger, the Kid had had his fill of gunfighting. At the war's conclusion he had promptly left New Mexico and headed north.

Unfortunately, Kid Sawyer's reputation had travelled with him. On his way northwards into Colorado, he had so far encountered no fewer than three young bucks keen to earn the reputation that the Kid was so anxious to lose. But he had no wish to die and, consequently, had been obliged to stand up to, and gun down, each in turn. And so, ironically, his reputation had continued to grow.

He had taken to avoiding towns and living off the land. As a crack shot, Kid Sawyer had had no trouble in feeding himself, for the forests and mountains of Colorado were teeming with game. Yet it was a lonely existence and the Kid, who had originally come from the bustling city of San Antonio, was by nature gregarious and not at all happy with only his own company. He craved the fellowship of others and, after a couple of months of solitude, had determined to chance riding into another town. Perhaps, he prayed, he might not be recognized.

The problem was Kid Sawyer's attire. It was far too distinctive, but, to date, he had had no opportunity to change it. Before he could do so, he had been challenged and then, immediately following the resulting gunfight, had left town. It was his intention, upon entering the next town, to call at the local dry goods store and purchase a change of clothes. For the moment, however, he was dressed from head to toe in black: low-crowned Stetson, buckskin gloves, leather vest, shirt, kerchief, denim pants and boots. And he was toting a pair of matched, pearl-handled forty-five calibre British Tranters, while in his saddleboot there rested a well-oiled Winchester rifle. Clad and armed in this fashion, Kid Sawyer was unlikely to achieve anonymity.

He had broken camp at dawn and had neither paused nor stopped since. It was now early evening and becoming dusky. Both horse and rider were nearly exhausted. Kid Sawyer peered anxiously ahead as the town came into view. Although not yet quite dark, several kerosene lamps had been lit in both houses and stores throughout the town. The Kid observed from the signpost he passed, as he crossed the town limits and rode into the settlement, that it was named Rifle. Not somewhere he had ever heard of. He had simply followed the river in the hope that, sooner or later, it would lead him to a place of human habitation.

Main Street was little different to a thousand others in small townships scattered across the West. It boasted one hotel, one saloon, a branch of the Cattlemen's Bank, a Court House, a blacksmith's forge, livery stables and several stores. Kid Sawyer noted that no light showed in the windows of the dry goods store and that a sign hanging inside the shop's glass-panelled front door bore the one word: *Closed.*

The Kid smiled wryly. He would have to chance his luck, since there was no way he could change his attire until the following morning when the dry goods store re-opened. He drew up beside a water trough and allowed the mare to quench her thirst. Then he trotted across to the Fast Buck Saloon, where he dismounted and hitched her to the rail outside. Before he rode her back to the livery stables, which he had passed on his way into town, he intended to quench his own raging thirst with a glass of cold beer. That the mare badly needed currying, food and rest, Kid Sawyer was well aware, but he figured that she could wait a few minutes. He clattered up the short flight of wooden steps onto the stoop and, pushing open the batwing doors, entered the saloon.

The Fast Buck Saloon consisted of one large barroom, with stairs at one end leading to the bedchambers upstairs, where the saloon's sporting women entertained their customers. Downstairs in the bar-room was a long, solid mahogany counter and several tables and chairs; the whole place was brightly lit by lamps hanging from the rafters. Blackjack and poker were the two games of chance on offer, and both seemed mighty popular, for there were no spare seats to be had round these tables. At the other tables sat a mixture of townsfolk, cowboys and homesteaders, happily drinking and chatting to those of the sporting women who were not presently engaged upstairs. Kid Sawyer pushed his way through the crowd standing three-deep at the bar and ordered himself a beer.

Behind the bar were the saloonkeeper, Rick

Rogers, and his bartender, Gus Brown. Both were busily occupied in serving the needs of the Fast Buck's numerous thirsty customers.

Rick Rogers was a tall, lean, dark-haired man in his early fifties. Shrewd grey eyes peered out from above an aquiline nose. His harsh, cadaverous face was clean-shaven except for a neat pencil-thin moustache and, despite having to tend to the constant demands of the drinkers, he kept a watchful eye over all sections of the bar-room. In his dark grey city-style suit, sparkling white shirt and black bootlace tie, he was easily the most elegant figure in the saloon. Beside him, stocky, bald-headed Gus Brown, in white shirt and black apron, perspired copiously as he struggled to pour the drinks fast enough. And it was Gus who served Kid Sawyer.

While Gus was handing the young gunslinger his change, Donny Bailey swaggered into the bar-room. Rick Rogers frowned; Donny Bailey was usually trouble. He was about the same age as Kid Sawyer, but, whereas the Kid, despite his participation in the Lincoln County range war, had retained his youthful good looks, Bailey's countenance had a debauched, sullen mien. The son of a wealthy rancher, Donny Bailey had been spoilt from childhood and had become, in his early twenties, a vindictive, cruel and totally self-regarding individual. He had no morals, no finer feelings and no respect for anyone.

A gambler, who cut up rough when he lost, and a womanizer, who treated the women whom he seduced with brutal contempt, Bailey had few friends.

Those he did have were, like himself, a bunch of no-account riff-raff. Indeed, they had encouraged him in his depravities and, when he had taken it into his head that he was something of a hot-shot with a handgun, they had urged him into settling his quarrels by means of a shoot-out. As a result of this, Donny Bailey had challenged and gunned down several of his contemporaries, two of whom had died. In recent weeks all of his acquaintances had taken good care not to rile him as he strutted about the town, arrogantly boasting that he was the fastest gun in the State of Colorado. So far, nobody had contradicted him.

A little over six foot tall, Bailey swaggered across the bar-room towards the long bar. He wore a grey Stetson, check shirt, Levis and unspurred boots and he had a sheepskin coat draped across his brawny shoulders. A Remington revolver was tied down to his right thigh. His fingers hovered menacingly a few inches above the Remington's butt. This fact did not go unnoticed, and a path opened before him as the Fast Buck's customers stepped aside to let him through.

Donny Bailey had been talking to one of his ne'er-do-well pals outside Rifle's general store when Kid

Sawyer rode into town. Upon his friend exclaiming that the newcomer was none other than the legendary gunfighter, Bailey's curiosity had been aroused and he had decided to follow the Kid into the saloon.

He planted himself next to the Kid and ordered a whiskey. And, while Gus Brown was pouring his drink, he quietly eyed Kid Sawyer up and down. The Kid was dressed exactly as Bailey expected, but his fresh features, medium height and slender build combined to make him seem a great deal less threatening and dangerous than his reputation suggested. Bailey took a quick slug of the whiskey. He finished it in two gulps, slammed the empty glass down on to the mahogany bartop and rasped, 'Same again.'

A nervous Gus Brown glanced at his boss. The saloonkeeper forced a thin smile and nodded.

'Yessir,' said the bartender, and he promptly poured a generous measure of the amber liquid into Donny Bailey's glass.

Bailey sipped the whiskey and turned towards the Kid.

'A friend of mine tells me you're the notorious Kid Sawyer,' he said.

The Kid's smile was as thin as Rick Rogers' had been.

'Yup,' he replied.

'You got quite a reputation,' stated Bailey.

'Yup.'

'You don't look like no goddam shootist to me.'

'No?'

'Nope.'

'Aw, hell, Donny! What's a shootist supposed to look like, anyway?' interjected the saloonkeeper, a worried frown creasing his brow.

'Tough. Manly.'

'Like you?' enquired the Kid.

'Yeah. Like me. Jest like me,' snarled Bailey.

'Wa'al, guess I'm the exception proves the rule,' remarked Kid Sawyer equably.

'I don't think so.'

'Oh, come now, Donny, there ain't no need to—' began the saloonkeeper anxiously.

'Keep outa this, Mr Rogers. I'm talkin' to the Kid,' said Bailey, and he fixed the saloon owner with a baleful glare.

Rogers took the hint and turned his attention to a waiting customer. He feared the worst, however, for unlike the rancher's son, he knew from experience that looks could be deceptive.

Donny Bailey, on the other hand, perceived the Kid's evident reluctance to engage him in a quarrel and mistakenly took this to be cowardice on the other's part. Consequently, he pressed on.

'I guess mebbe your reputation is a mite exaggerated,' he said contemptuously.

14

'That so?'

'You don't deny it?'

'I neither deny nor confirm it.' Kid Sawyer's tone was mild, yet his blue eyes were suddenly ice-cold. 'I don't care to talk 'bout my reputation, if it's all the same to you?'

Bailey laughed, a harsh, mirthless laugh.

'But it ain't all the same to me,' he sneered.

By now Bailey had convinced himself that Kid Sawyer's reputation was indeed exaggerated. He told himself that the ranchers embroiled in the Lincoln County range war had engaged professional shootists like the Kid to fight on their behalf, simply because their cowpokes were no gunfighters. And so, he concluded, the Kid's reputation was based solely on his having gunned down a few hapless ranch-hands. Bailey smiled. He intended that he should be known, not only as the fastest gun in the State of Colorado, but also as the man who had challenged and killed the notorious Kid Sawyer.

The Kid, meantime, had finished his beer and placed the glass on the bar counter.

'Same again?' enquired Gus Brown, hoping to diffuse the situation.

Rick Rogers glanced at the bartender and nodded approvingly, but Kid Sawyer shook his head.

'I don't think so,' he replied, and he turned as though to leave the bar-room.

As he did so, Donny Bailey stepped in front of him.

'That reputation of yourn . . .' he began.

'Ain't none of your goddam business,' snapped the Kid.

Bailey blinked. The other's demeanour had altered dramatically. The colour had left the Kid's face and his youthful countenance had assumed an expression that was both harsh and uncompromising.

'Now I don't take at all kindly to bein' spoken to like that,' blustered Bailey, taken aback by the other's sudden change of tone.

'No?'

'Nope. I was jest makin' conversation. But I guess you didn't like me suggestin' you ain't quite the hotshot you claim to be.'

'You wanta back up that suggestion?' asked Kid Sawyer coolly. 'If not, git outa my way. I need to go tend to my hoss.'

In that instant Donny Bailey knew he had made a bad mistake. But all eyes were on him. He dared not back down. The other drinkers at the bar had moved away. He and the Kid stood facing each other. Behind the counter, Rick Rogers and the bartender stood motionless, nervously watching the events unfold and evidently unwilling to intervene.

Both young men backed off a few paces and, when

they were approximately twenty feet apart, halted. An uncanny silence had descended upon the bar-room. Nobody moved. Then, all at once, Donny Bailey dropped his hand onto the butt of his Remington. As he swiftly pulled the revolver clear of its holster, so, too, did Kid Sawyer draw the .45 calibre British Tranters. All three guns blazed and both men went down.

Donny Bailey's shot struck the Kid high up on his left shoulder, breaking his collarbone and knocking him clean off his feet. Bailey was not so lucky. The slugs from the Tranters struck him in the chest and smashed through his body, exiting out of his back in a stream of blood and splintered bone. By the time he hit the floorboards, his check shirt was stained crimson and he was already dead.

Kid Sawyer, who had momentarily passed out, was picked up and settled in a chair near the bar. When eventually he recovered consciousness, he found Rick Rogers standing over him, together with the representatives of the law in Rifle, namely Sheriff John Jarvis and his deputy, Tim Waite. The former was a large, red-faced bear of a man, the latter a tall, gangling fellow in his early twenties.

Sheriff Jarvis indicated, with a jerk of his thumb, the spread-eagled body of Donny Bailey, stretched out on the bar-room floor.

'You shoot that feller?' he rasped.

The Kid glanced from the lawman to the corpse and sighed.

'I guess so,' he said quietly.

'In that case, I'm arrestin' you for the murder of—' Jarvis began.

'Hey, hang on one minute, Sheriff! I didn't murder him. It was a fair fight.'

'I recognize you, *Mister* Sawyer. You're a noted shootist.'

'So?'

'So, you come into this here town an' pick a quarrel with one of our citizens an' shoot him dead. I call that murder, what with you bein' a professional gunman an' him—'

'Bein' a braggart an' a bully an' lookin' for trouble,' interjected Rick Rogers.

The sheriff rounded on the saloonkeeper.

'What are yuh sayin', Mr Rogers?' he demanded hotly.

'I'm sayin' it was Donny who picked the fight, not the Kid,' declared Rogers.

'That's right, Sheriff,' averred Gus Brown from behind the bar.

Half a dozen other voices were raised in agreement. Donny Bailey might have been a local man, but he was far from popular. Indeed, given his argumentative manner and his penchant for challenging folks to duels, most of those present were mightily

18

relieved to see him dead.

The sheriff scowled. He detested professional gun-slingers and had been only too keen to charge Kid Sawyer with Bailey's murder. Now it seemed he was to be denied this opportunity.

'Wa'al, I dunno . . .' he growled.

'Aw, c'mon, Sheriff! You won't git no conviction. 'Deed, I expect Judge Hawkins'll throw the case outa court an' lambast you for wastin' his time,' said Rogers.

Sheriff Jarvis continued to scowl. Nevertheless, he realized that what the saloonkeeper said was undoubtedly true. The judge was noted for his iras-cibility and he, Jarvis, had no wish to be the object of it.

'OK,' he muttered, 'there will be no charge.'

'We had best call Doc Barnard over to tend to the Kid's wound,' said Rogers. 'Perhaps Tim could go fetch him?'

'Sure thing, Mr Rogers,' said the young deputy.

'Oh, no!' rasped Jarvis, grabbing hold of Tim Waite's arm and restraining him.

'But, Sheriff, he's bleedin' bad an' . . .' protested Rogers.

'No, Mr Rogers. His kind are trouble.' Jarvis turned to Kid Sawyer and snapped, 'I want you outa town. Now.'

The Kid opened his mouth to protest, but upon

encountering the sheriff's implacable gaze, he saw that to do so would be useless.

'OK,' he said. 'Jest gimme a minute.'

Rick Rogers offered him a large whiskey, which Gus Brown had passed across the counter. The Kid shook his head.

'No, thanks. Let me have a glass of water. Please.'

This was quickly produced and the young gunfighter proceeded to gulp it down. Then he slowly rose to his feet. His face was chalk-white and he staggered and almost fell. Tim Waite and Rick Rogers grabbed hold of him and held him upright. The blood from his shoulder wound continued to seep through his shirt, the loss of which was causing him to feel faint.

'Surely we oughta patch up that there wound 'fore we send him on his way?' said Rogers.

John Jarvis's face darkened.

'No,' said the sheriff. 'The sonofabitch can find hisself a doctor some place else.'

'But the next town's a good twenty miles away!' protested Rogers.

'Git him outa here!'

The saloonkeeper shrugged his shoulders. There was no gainsaying the peace officer. Sheriff Jarvis was a hard, hard man and not someone anybody in Rifle was eager to cross. But Rogers had to admit the sheriff was also a brave and honest fellow, one who exercised the law in Rifle without fear or favour.

Rogers and the deputy half-carried the weakened gunfighter across the bar-room and through the batwing doors out on to the stoop. They helped Kid Sawyer down the steps and across to the hitching rail, where they lifted him up onto his black mare. While the Kid was slowly, painfully clambering into the saddle, Sheriff John Jarvis headed for the livery stables. His piebald was kept there. He would needs saddle the horse and set out to Sam Bailey's spread, where he proposed to break the news of his son's death to the rancher. Not a task he was looking forward to.

Kid Sawyer took hold of the reins and urged the mare in an easterly direction along Main Street. The exhausted animal was quite unable to raise even a trot and, consequently, their progress was incredibly slow. A few lights shone out from the stores and houses which the Kid passed. The dusk deepened. Ahead of him, at the edge of the town, he could dimly discern the dark mass of the local church, with its steeple. Directly opposite stood the pastor's house, a large, two-storey frame building. In stark contrast to the church, lights were blazing forth from all of its windows.

It was as the Kid drew level with both the church and the pastor's house that his remaining strength ebbed away and he slipped from the saddle, to sprawl senseless on the ground. The mare straightway halted beside her fallen rider. That end of the town was quite deserted, but Kid Sawyer was in luck. His fall from the mare's back had been spotted by the wife of the pastor, the Reverend Nick Hollis.

A slim, pretty young woman in her late twenties, Annie Hollis was the mother of two daughters, Laurie aged eight and Jane, seven. She had been putting the two girls to bed and, just before drawing shut their bedroom curtains, had heard the sound of a horse's hoofs and glanced out of the window. As she did so, Kid Sawyer toppled out of the saddle. Annie gasped, quickly closed the curtains and, telling her daughters that she would be back in a minute to read them their bedtime story, hurried off downstairs.

The Reverend Nick Hollis was still sitting at the dining table, finishing a second cup of coffee. The clergyman, a tall, handsome 30-year-old sombrely dressed in clerical garb, looked up in surprise as his wife suddenly burst into the room.

'Nick! Nick! There's a man outside who's fallen from his horse!' she exclaimed.

'Drunk?' enquired the pastor.

'I . . . I don't know. He's lying awful still. I think you'd best go look. He might jest be ill.'

Hollis hastily finished his coffee and rose from the table.

'OK,' he said. 'You head back upstairs. I'll go see what's what.'

Annie smiled nervously.

'You be careful, Nick,' she murmured.

'I will. Don't worry.'

The pastor went outside and cautiously approached the fallen rider. Observing that Kid Sawyer did not stir, he crouched down beside him. Immediately, he noted the youthful countenance, its deathly pallor and the blood seeping from the bullet-hole in the Kid's shoulder.

Nick Hollis recognized the need to tend to the wound without delay, for it was obvious that the youngster had lost a lot of blood. If he lost much more, it could prove fatal. Quickly, Hollis slipped one arm behind the Kid's back and the other beneath his knees. Then he staggered to his feet, with the Kid in his arms, and carried him into the house.

While Annie read to her daughters upstairs, her husband stripped Kid Sawyer of his shirt and vest and cleansed the wound as best he could. He soon saw that the bullet had broken the collarbone and passed straight through the shoulder. Using a fresh towel, he eventually succeeded in staunching the bleeding.

Some minutes later, leaving Laurie and Jane fast asleep, Annie came downstairs. It was while she and the pastor were discussing how the Kid might have come by his wound that Kid Sawyer regained his senses.

'Wh . . . where am I?' he gasped, as he looked about him in some bewilderment.

The Reverend Nick Hollis smiled.

'You're in Rifle, in my house opposite the church,' he said and then, by way of explanation, he added, 'I'm the local pastor and this is my wife.'

Annie also smiled.

'I saw you fall from your horse and Nick brought you inside,' she said.

'Yes. I've temporarily patched up your wound,' stated Hollis. 'But I'd like to know how you came by it.'

'Ah!'

'Come on. Tell us,' urged the pastor.

'You won't like what I have to tell you,' replied the Kid. 'You see, I've jest killed a man.'

Annie gasped, while her husband continued to regard the youngster with a cool, dispassionate eye.

'I think you'd best explain,' he said quietly.

'OK,' said the Kid. 'It was like this. . . .' And he went on to recount what had happened at the Fast Buck Saloon, remarking that, since his participation in the Lincoln County range war, his fame had tempted a number of would-be shootists to challenge him.

'Dressed all in black as you are, I guess you'd be

instantly recognizable,' commented Hollis.

'Yeah. Which is why, when I rode into Rifle, I aimed to buy me a new set of clothes. Unfortunately, I found the dry goods store to be closed.'

'I see.'

'Anyway, what's done is done. So, if you could bind up the wound, I'd be obliged to you an' be on my way.'

'Oh, no!' exclaimed Hollis. 'That wound needs tending to by a proper medical man, and, besides, your collarbone is broken and must be re-set.'

'That's right,' agreed Annie. And, turning to the pastor, she said, 'Go fetch Charles.'

'Charles?' enquired the Kid.

'Doctor Charles Barnard. He lives next door.'

'But the sheriff said—'

'It's OK. Charles is a good friend. He will, I am sure, be prepared to treat you and keep the matter secret.'

'Yes. Sheriff Jarvis need never know,' said Hollis.

'And you will stay with us until you are fit to travel,' declared Annie emphatically.

'You . . . you're prepared to give refuge to me, a worthless gunslinger!' exclaimed an astonished Kid Sawyer.

'Nobody is worthless,' retorted the pastor. 'You said that you were going to buy a new set of clothes. I assume, therefore, that it is your intention to give up the gun and make a new life for yourself?'

'Yes. That's so,' confirmed the Kid.

'Then, it is our Christian duty to help you,' said Hollis.

'It certainly is,' averred Annie.

'I'll go fetch Charles, then I'll see to your horse. It can be kept alongside ours in the stables at the back of the house. Then, when you are fit and ready to move on, you can leave town, with nobody any the wiser,' said Hollis.

Kid Sawyer smiled wanly. His luck had changed dramatically. Although very weak from the loss of blood, he felt his spirits rise. The future seemed suddenly quite bright.

# AUGUST 1885

# TWO

A burning sun beat down on the group of horsemen as they approached the small, dusty town of Steamboat Springs, Colorado. There were seven of them in total. Their leader was Blair Wilton, a man utterly devoid of any redeeming features whatsoever. A ruthless killer, a pitiless rapist and a violent robber, Wilton was feared far and wide across the West. His ugly features decorated 'Most Wanted' posters across no fewer than eight states from Texas up to Colorado, where he and his gang were presently operating.

Cruel, ice-cold blue eyes peered out from an unshaven, pockmarked face. Wilton's nose had been broken and flattened, and he bore long, livid scars on both cheeks, the legacy of a knife-fight in which he had killed a man. His mouth was twisted into a perpetual sneer and there was no hint of humour in those ice-cold blue eyes. He wore a wide-brimmed brown Stetson and, despite the heat, a rather thread-bare Prince Albert coat. He was riding a black stallion and carried a Colt Peacemaker, in a holster tied down on his right thigh, and a Colt Hartford revolving rifle in his saddleboot.

The other six gang members were no more pre-possessing than their leader. Frank and Hank Pearson were cousins who could have been taken for brothers. Squat, mean-eyed, beetle-browed and heavily bearded, they, too, wore brown Stetsons, though neither dressed in a Prince Albert coat. Instead, they both wore brown leather vests over well-worn check shirts. Each cousin rode a pinto and their weapons matched Blair Wilton's exactly.

Kenny Shaw, Deadeye Drummond and Larry Snaith were similarly attired, only the checks and the colours of their Stetsons differing. Kenny Shaw, a tall, lean, lantern-jawed Texan, with a drooping Mexican-style moustache, carried a Colt Peacemaker and a Winchester, while Deadeye Drummond, a small, squint-eyed weasel of a man, and Larry Snaith, tall, blond, broad-shouldered and handsome, preferred Remington revolvers and, like their chief, Colt Hartford rifles. All three rode chestnut mares.

The seventh man was an Easterner, clad in a grey Derby hat and grey three-piece, city-style suit. His face was pale and podgy and his vest stretched tightly over his girth. Fat and flabby, Gil Ambrose was not a natural horseman and was finding the ride something of an ordeal. He sat astride a very docile grey gelding and his weapon of choice was a long-barrelled .30 calibre Colt, carried in a shoulder-rig beneath his jacket.

The gang had met up some weeks earlier, across the state line in Wyoming, at a notorious hell-hole named Providence Flats.

There were several similar townships dotted across the West, where the law dared not venture and where desperate men with a price on their heads could hide out, safe from the fear of capture. In such places they could rest until the hue and cry died down and it was time to set forth on some further nefarious venture.

These towns boasted saloons and bordellos in plenty, livery stables and usually a funeral parlour, but no law office and no church. Providence Flats was no exception, although it did have an hotel, a run-down, two-storey frame building that was most inappropriately named the Grand Hotel.

The Golden Garter was the largest saloon in town and by far and away the most popular. It was owned by a one-time bank robber named Frank Cassidy, who found fleecing his fellow desperadoes far easier and a deal more profitable than bank robbery had ever been. And it was in the Golden Garter's huge bar-room-cum-gaming hall that the seven outlaws had met and formed themselves into a gang under Blair Wilton's leadership.

The Pearson cousins, Kenny Shaw, Deadeye Drummond and Larry Snaith had all, in their time, tried their hands at both cattle-rustling and holding up stagecoaches, sometimes on their own and sometimes not. None had been particularly successful. Neither had Gil Ambrose in his career as a professional burglar. His last job had ended in disaster when he had been disturbed by the householder. He had shot and killed the man, who turned out to be related to the local mayor. Consequently, Ambrose had immediately left town and headed out West.

Since the six were fast running out of money and undecided what to do next, Blair Wilton had had no difficulty in recruiting them into his gang. He had been a little dubious about taking on Gil Ambrose, but, as seven was his lucky number, had relented and included the fat Easterner.

So far, the Wilton gang had attempted only stagecoach hold-ups, with limited success. The takings on each occasion had been poor. Now they were aiming to rob a bank. The First National Bank in Steamboat Springs was to be their target. But they had not thought to reconnoitre the town.

'We'll jest ride in, stick up the bank an' be on our way 'fore they know what's hit 'em,' Blair Wilton had declared confidently.

31

Such had been their briefing. Meticulous planning was not Blair Wilton's forte.

It was mid-afternoon when, eventually, the gang crossed the town limits and entered Steamboat Springs. They trotted slowly down the town's hot and dusty Main Street. Few people were about. Most were indoors, sensibly avoiding the heat of the sun.

Blair Wilton scanned the sidewalks and the buildings that lined Main Street. Presently, he spotted the bank and, next to it, the law office. This was scarcely the perfect set-up, he mused. Yet he was in luck. The rocking chair, which stood on the sidewalk immediately in front of the law office, was empty. Evidently, the town marshal had decided it was too hot to sit outside.

The seven rode up to the bank and dismounted. They then proceeded to hitch their horses to the rail provided for the bank's customers.

'OK,' growled Wilton. 'Let's git goin'.' He turned to Larry Snaith and said, 'You stay out here with the hosses, Larry. If 'n the marshal or his deppities should put in an appearance, you holler.'

'Sure thing, boss,' replied Snaith.

The outlaws pulled up their kerchiefs, to cover the lower part of their faces, and then their chief led the charge into the bank. The others piled in behind him, Gil Ambrose bringing up the rear. As they erupted through its doors, they hastily drew and brandished their revolvers. Inside, the bank manager and his teller were dealing with a couple of customers.

Lawrence Dove, the manager, was the first to glance up and see the outlaws. The colour promptly drained from his face. Tall and elegant, with fine, aristocratic features, Dove looked the part in his black frock coat, sparkling white linen shirt and grey cravat. There was no mistaking who was the manager and who the teller. His assistant, Sammy Gordon, was a thin, spotty-faced youth attired in a rather ill-fitting brown suit. The teller's face, too, was now chalk-white, and large, frightened eyes peered nervously from behind his wire-framed spectacles.

As for the bank's two customers, one was Lizzie Lang, the 40-year-old wife of a homesteader, a short, pretty, dark-haired woman in a gingham gown and broad-brimmed straw hat. The other was Fred Tench, a local storekeeper. He had put on his Sunday best in order to create a good impression, since he was visiting the bank with the intention of requesting a loan. The appearance of the outlaws, however, chased any thought of business from his mind. All he wanted now was to escape.

While Lizzie Lang screamed, he turned and dashed towards the door, elbowing both Deadeye Drummond and Gil Ambrose aside. He had just reached the open doorway when Hank Pearson swung round and fired. Two .45 calibre slugs slammed into Tench's back, throwing him forwards through the doorway and on to the sidewalk. He twitched for a moment or two and then lay motionless, spread-eagled across the wooden boards.

Meantime, Lizzie continued to scream until Blair Wilton stepped across and clubbed her senseless with the barrel of his Colt Peacemaker. As she collapsed to the floor, Wilton turned his attention to the bank manager and his young teller.

'OK,' Wilton yelled at Sammy Gordon. 'You fill some bags with any money you've got stashed behind that counter. An' you,' he snarled at Lawrence Dove, 'open up your goddam safe!'

'No!' cried Dove defiantly. 'I won't do it!'

'N . . . nor me,' added Gordon, though he trembled as he spoke.

'Yes, you darned well will!' roared Wilton and, lifting the flap at the far end of the counter, he slipped behind it and grabbed hold of the manager.

Deadeye Drummond swiftly followed his leader and threw himself upon the teller.

But the two bank officials were not to be so easily overcome. Fearing for their lives, they fought like wildcats and, in the mêlée that followed, were giving as good as they got when Frank Pearson and Kenny Shaw crept up behind them and, reversing their guns, dealt them each a sickening blow to the back of the skull. Like Lizzie Lang before them, Lawrence Dove and Sammy Gordon sank senseless to the floor. At that same moment, there came the sound of shooting from outside the bank.

'Jeez, we gotta git outa here!' cried Hank Pearson.

'Sure have!' agreed an anxious Gil Ambrose, his pale, podgy face a shade whiter than usual.

'Not before we grab some of this cash,' rasped Blair Wilton.

'But boss . . .' began Deadeye Drummond.

'Shuddup an' start shovin' them notes into one of these canvas bags,' said Wilton.

He had found the bags next to the two counter drawers, both of which contained a supply of various denominations of banknotes. He chucked one bag at Drummond and began ramming one, five, ten and twenty dollar bills into the other.

Meantime, outside the bank, Larry Snaith suddenly found himself confronting the forces of law and order in the persons of Marshal Jake Lawley and Deputies Bart Nugent and Jim Masters. Hank Pearson's shots had alerted the three peace officers, Marshal Lawley and Deputy Nugent emerging from the law office and Deputy Masters from the barbering parlour further down the street. All three were brandishing Colt Peacemakers and each had his badge of office pinned to his chest.

As Larry Snaith made a grab for his revolver, the

marshal yelled, 'Hands up, you sonofabitch!'

Snaith scowled and, ignoring the lawman's order, pulled the gun from its holster. He was in the act of aiming at Lawley when the three peace officers simultaneoulsy opened fire. Two shots from Lawley and one each from his deputies slammed into the outlaw's chest, sending him crashing backwards among the horses hitched to the rail outside the bank. The horses whinnied, neighed and desperately attempted to pull free from the rail. In so doing, they trampled upon the fallen outlaw, who, in any case, was dying from his wounds. As their hoofs pounded him and the blood spewed out from the gaping bullet holes in his chest, Larry Snaith gasped his last breath.

By this time, several more of Steamboat Springs' citizens had converged upon the scene, armed with shotguns, rifles and revolvers. They crouched in doorways and open windows, and behind water troughs, buckboards, wagons and barrels containing flour, salted meats and other provisions.

Consequently, when Kenny Shaw led the charge out of the bank, he was met with a veritable barrage of shots. His head and body were riddled with bullets, the blood spurting out of him as though from a colander.

Behind him, Gil Ambrose hastily threw himself down on to the sidewalk and scrambled along on his knees, before diving into the midst of the horses. Hank Pearson followed suit, while his cousin Frank, together with Blair Wilton and Deadeye Drummond, rushed forward, firing off their guns as they ran. Their rapid gunfire forced the lawmen to drop to the ground and various other citizens to duck down behind the nearest barrier.

This gave the bank robbers a chance to unhitch and mount their horses. And, as they hurriedly swung into their saddles, the outlaws continued to fire away at the peace officers and townsfolk, all of whom promptly returned fire.

In the gun battle that followed, Gil Ambrose succeeded in hitting Deputy Bart Nugent in the right arm, causing him to drop his gun. At the same time, Blair Wilton and Deadeye Drummond gunned down two of the nearest townsfolk. Wilton's shot penetrated the heart of Steamboat Springs' blacksmith, when he unwisely popped up from behind a water trough, and Drummond blasted one of its storekeeper's brains out of the back of his skull as he stood in a doorway opposite, reloading his shotgun.

Moments later, the five surviving members of the Wilton gang were racing back along Main Street in the direction from which they had come. Behind them Marshal Jake Lawley, Deputy Jim Masters and various citizens blazed away at their retreating figures. But none of their shots found its target; Blair

Wilton and his four henchmen succeeded in crossing the town limits unscathed. The outlaws had, however, little to show for their raid. Most of the bank's cash remained in its safe. Only a very small proportion of its banknotes had been residing in the drawers behind the counter.

Blair Wilton swore roundly as he led the others north across the plain towards the distant state line. His plan now was to cross back into Wyoming and hide out again in Providence Flats, there to rest up and decide upon their next venture. The gang's takings from stagecoach hold-ups had been poor and those from this, their first bank robbery, no better. In consequence, Blair Wilton was not a happy man. He realized that, if he were to keep his gang together, the next enterprise needs must be a great deal more profitable.

Meantime, back in Steamboat Springs, Marshal Jake Lawley was counting the cost of the raid. He and his two deputies stood in the centre of Main Street and stared at the corpses littering its sidewalks and thoroughfare. As they did so, the town's mortician approached the fallen blacksmith and its doctor headed towards the wounded deputy.

Jake Lawley, a slim, granite-faced man in his mid-forties, glanced at his deputies, Bart Nugent, young and fresh-complexioned, and Jim Masters, the oldest of the three, a sprightly, grey-haired fifty-year-old. He regarded the younger man with an anxious eye.

'You're bleedin' bad,' he commented tersely.

Bart Nugent smiled bravely and shook his head.

'I'm OK, Marshal,' he replied. 'It's only a flesh wound. The sonofabitch jest nicked me.'

'Wa'al, you git the doc to tend to it,' growled Lawley.

'That's exactly what I'm gonna do, Jake,' said Doc Manning, as he approached them. 'You're losin' blood fast, Bart,' he informed the young deputy.

While the doctor set about staunching Bart Nugent's wound, Marshal Lawley turned to Jim Masters.

'There's three of our townsfolk dead that I can see,' he said grimly. 'C'mon, let's mosey on over to the bank an' find out what's what in there.'

'Good idea, Marshal,' said the deputy.

Both men feared the worst and, therefore, they were mightily relieved to find both Lawrence Dove and his teller alive and occupied with ministering to a decidedly groggy Lizzie Lang. The three of them had lumps, bruises and abrasions to their skulls and raging headaches, all of which would require Doc Manning's attention. But thankfully none had sustained a mortal wound.

'What happened outside?' enquired Lawrence Dove. 'Did you manage to gun down those murderin' varmints?'

'A couple of 'em,' said Lawley. 'I'm afraid the rest escaped. How much did they take, Mr Dove?'

The bank manager shrugged his shoulders.

'I dunno for sure. Sammy an' I'll need to check.' He smiled dourly and added, 'I don't figure they took too much. Only what little we had in the drawers behind the counter.'

'That's right,' said Sammy Gordon. 'The vast majority of the cash was locked away in the safe.'

'They didn't force you to open that, then?' said Jake Lawley.

'No, they didn't,' replied Dove.

'Five men dead, an' for what?' rasped the marshal.

'So, they killed two more 'sides Fred Tench?' murmured Dove.

'Yeah. A bad business altogether,' said Lawley sadly.

'D'you know who the bastards were?' demanded Dove.

'I do,' said Lawley. 'A coupla their masks slipped an' I recognized 'em: Blair Wilton an' Deadeye Drummond.'

'The Wilton gang!' exclaimed Sammy Gordon. 'I read 'bout them in the newspapers. But I thought they was specializin' in holdin' up stagecoaches!'

'There's certainly been a spate of hold-ups across the state that were blamed on Blair Wilton an' his gang,' said the marshal.

'Wa'al, I guess they decided to try their hand at a bank robbery for a change,' said Masters.

'Yeah.'

'So, Marshal, you gonna whip up a posse an' git after them?' asked Lizzie Lang, entering the conversation for the first time.

Marshal Lawley smiled at the pretty little homesteader's wife and shook his head.

'No; there'd be no point. They've got too good a lead on us. There's no chance we'd catch 'em.'

'But surely you can do somethin'?' remarked Lawrence Dove.

'If I can figure out roughly where they're headed, I could warn the townships in an' around that territory.'

'They were headin' west when they left town,' said Jim Masters. 'If they continue westward, that'll take 'em across the state line into Utah an' towards the Uinta Mountains. A good place to hide out.'

'Or they could turn north and make for Wyoming,' pointed out Lizzie.

'Or south an' . . .' began the deputy.

'I'll go find out which,' stated Lawley. 'An' I'll leave you, Jim, to see to things back here in town. OK?'

'Yeah, Marshal. I'll take care of everythin',' affirmed the deputy.

'Good. I'll be on my way, then. An' I'll ask the doc

to pop in an' see to you folks once he's finished tendin' Bart.'

A look of alarm spread across Lizzie's face.

'Young Bart's been hurt?' she asked anxiously.

'A flesh wound. He'll be fine,' the marshal reassured her.

Then he was gone.

He made straight for the livery stables, where he kept his horse, a brown gelding. It took only a few minutes for him to saddle and mount his horse, whereupon he set off at a brisk canter in the wake of the outlaws.

Tracking the Wilton gang across the plain proved fairly easy. The marshal observed that, a couple of miles out of town, they had turned northwards. It seemed, therefore, that they were heading for Wyoming. However, Lawley wanted to be absolutely sure. Consequently, he continued to follow their tracks for a further six miles. Then, since Blair Wilton and his confederates remained steadfastly northbound, he pulled up, convinced they did indeed mean to cross over from Colorado into Wyoming. He turned the gelding's head and slowly trotted back towards Steamboat Springs.

# THREE

Blair Wilton and his gang crossed the state line into Wyoming and reached Providence Flats a few days later. Having left their horses at the livery stables to be curried, fed and rested, the outlaws made their way to the Grand Hotel, where they booked accommodation for the night and filled their hungry bellies.

Rested and well fed, they then crossed the street to the Golden Garter. Tomorrow would be soon enough to make plans for the future. Tonight would be given over solely to drinking, fornicating and gambling.

Inside the huge bar-room-cum-gaming hall, tobacco smoke swirled round in thick eddies, diluting the light cast by the numerous kerosene lamps hanging from the rafters. On a small stage, a girl in a low-cut scarlet dress sang to the accompaniment of a honky-tonk piano. The solid mahogany bar counter was awash with spilt beer and whiskey, and the four bartenders behind it were being kept busy, dealing with the constant demands of the large crowd of drinkers.

Frank Cassidy happily presided over these proceedings. He was a slim, swarthy-looking fellow, neatly attired in a black city-style suit, sparkling white shirt with a ruffled collar, black tie, dark-green brocade vest and highly polished black shoes. And he had about him an air of quiet authority.

As usual, Cassidy kept a vigilant eye on his customers, for he liked to nip trouble in the bud. And, so, he was quick to observe Blair Wilton and his gang swagger into the saloon. He relaxed, however, when he saw the five, after ordering beers, immediately disperse. Gil Ambrose and Frank and Hank Pearson each grabbed a sporting woman and headed upstairs, while Blair Wilton sat down at one of the saloon's three poker tables and Deadeye Drummond joined those gamblers who were trying their luck at the roulette wheel.

In this manner, the gang passed their evening at the Golden Garter. Both Wilton and Drummond succeeded in losing almost all their ill-gotten gains, while Ambrose and the Pearson cousins, once they had satisfied their carnal desires, proceeded to drink themselves into a stupor.

Therefore, the cousins and Gil Ambrose remained still abed when, very late the following morning, Blair Wilton and Deadeye Drummond returned to the saloon. They found that, where it had been packed out the previous night, now it had but a sprinkling of customers.

While Wilton was ordering a couple of beers, he spotted one of the gamblers with whom he had been playing poker. They exchanged wry smiles, for the other had fared no better than Wilton at the poker table.

'Let me buy those beers,' said the stranger and, extending his hand, he introduced himself: 'Paul Springer at your service.'

'Blair Wilton,' drawled the outlaw chief. 'An' this here's Dick Drummond, better known as Deadeye.'

The stranger lifted his glass.

'Your good health, gents,' he said.

'An' yours.'

'You've got yourself quite a reputation, Mr Wilton.'

Wilton carefully eyed the other man. What he saw was a slim, dark-haired man in his late thirties. Springer had slicked-back hair and a pencil-thin moustache, and he was dressed, like the saloon's proprietor, in a black city-style suit. He wore a grey Derby hat at a jaunty angle, and a pair of shrewd grey eyes peered out of his handsome, smiling face. Wilton

45

was, if nothing else, a pretty good judge of character and he knew a shyster when he saw one. In fact, Springer was just the kind of man Wilton was looking to recruit into his gang.

'I've had a li'l bad luck lately,' he confessed.

'Indeed?' said Springer.

'Yeah. We raided a bank some days back, but lost two men an' came away with precious little loot,' growled Deadeye Drummond.

'That a fact?'

'It is. C'mon over to that table in the corner an' I'll tell you all about it,' said Wilton.

'OK,' said a curious Paul Springer.

The three men carried their beers from the bar counter to the table which Blair Wilton had indicated. They sat down and, once Wilton had knocked back a good draught of his beer, he began to relate the story of the gang's raid on the First National Bank in Steamboat Springs. He left out nothing and concluded by saying, 'Holdin' up stages is one thing, robbin' a bank is somethin' else. The first is a pretty darned straightforward operation, the second needs careful plannin'. I confess I should've reconnoitred the town 'fore we rode in.'

Deadeye Drummond nodded his agreement.

'Next time we won't make that mistake,' he muttered.

'Trouble is, who do we send in to reconnoitre?

We're all wanted men,' growled the outlaw chief.

'Mebbe Gil . . .' began Drummond.

'Hell, no!' said Wilton. 'The feller's a none-too-clever, one-time burglar from the East coast. I took him on to make up numbers, but I don't reckon he'd be up to carryin' out no reconnaissance.'

'Wa'al, he's the only one of us who ain't likely to be recognized,' stated Drummond.

'Even so.'

'There's gonna be a next time then?' murmured Springer.

'Yup,' said Wilton. 'Later today, me an' the boys will git together an' decide when an' where.'

'The gang ain't splittin' up?'

'Nope. We jest figured on lammin' outa here to Providence Flats an' lyin' low for a while. Last night we had ourselves some fun. Today will be soon enough to make plans. Ain't that right, Deadeye?'

'Sure is, Blair,' replied Drummond amiably.

'Our number is reduced, though. From seven to five.' Wilton glanced quizzically at their new acquaintance. 'Care to join us, Mr Springer?' he enquired.

'I'm kinda like your pal, the one you called Gil. I ain't no Westerner,' stated Springer.

'From one of the East coast cities, are yuh?'

'Nope. Me, I'm from Chicago.'

'So, what brought you out West?'

'I got caught in bed with someone else's woman.'

'The wife of some Chicago dignitary, huh?'

'Worse'n that. The mistress of Big Tony Demarco, a gangster with a nasty habit of bumpin' off anyone who displeases him.' Paul Springer smiled and added drily, 'An' I sure as hell displeased him. Therefore, I decided to quit town pretty goddam quick.'

The two outlaws laughed and Wilton said, 'The offer remains open. You wanta ride with me an' the boys?'

Springer cogitated for a few moments, took a couple of swigs of his beer and smiled. 'OK,' he said. 'I'm your man. But, I warn you, I ain't no sharpshooter.'

'You can fire a gun, though, cain't yuh?' demanded Wilton.

'Oh, yeah.' Springer pulled aside his jacket to reveal an Army Model Colt nestling in its holster. 'From my Civil War days. I fought with General George H. Thomas at Chattanooga an' Nashville.'

'Did you now?'

'Yup. But I ain't done much shootin' since.'

'That's OK. It ain't a shootist I'm lookin' for.'

'No?'

'Nope. What I need is someone who can reconnoitre our next target without gittin' hisself arrested. Like I said, I don't figure Gil Ambrose is up to the task. Yet I reckon you could be.'

Springer nodded.

'Yeah, I guess I could do that,' he concurred.

'We'd need to know whereabouts the law office is located, if it's near the bank for instance. An' a description of the bank's layout, an' what kinda safe it's got, would be real helpful. Also—'

'Don't worry, I'll be sure to provide you with all the information you need,' said Springer.

Blair Wilton grinned. He felt certain that Paul Springer would do just that. The man was bright and he was confident, but not cocky. Wilton congratulated himself on having stumbled upon the very fellow he needed to ensure that the gang's next raid was a success.

'Glad to have you along,' he said.

'Jest one thing, though,' said Springer.

'Yeah?'

'Hows about carryin' a few sticks of dynamite with us next time. Then, if again you have trouble persuadin' the manager to open the safe, you can simply blast it open.'

'But that'd alert the townsfolk.'

'The shock of the explosion would surely delay 'em for some moments. Long enough for us to empty the safe an' be on our way.'

'Hmm. Mebbe,' muttered Blair Wilton doubtfully.

'Wouldn't do no harm carryin' a few sticks, Blair. Jest in case,' opined Deadeye Drummond.

'No. Guess not,' admitted Wilton. 'How many

49

d'you think we'd need, Paul?'

'A couple'd probably do the job. But let's say we take half a dozen.'

'OK, for, sure as hell, none of us is capable of crackin' a safe. Gil could likely pick a door lock, but I reckon that's 'bout his limit.' Wilton smiled sourly and remarked, 'I hope we don't need to use the dynamite, but if all else fails. . . .'

So it was agreed. Thereafter, the three men continued to talk and drink beer until the rest of Wilton's gang turned up at a little after noon. Then they straightway adjourned to a nearby cantina, where they feasted on chicken fajitas wrapped in soft tacos. And it was while they ate that Blair Wilton introduced the newcomer to the other three outlaws and explained what role he proposed Paul Springer should play in their forthcoming venture.

'Sounds good to me,' said Gil Ambrose.

'An' to me,' added Hank Pearson.

His cousin Frank nodded his agreement, before asking, 'Whereabouts you plannin' to raid, Blair? We pickin' on some township here in Wyomin', or are we headin' back down into Colorado?'

Wilton scratched his head.

'Don't rightly know,' he confessed.

'I vote we stay here in Wyomin'. We're too well known in Colorado, an' the forces of law an' order there will be sure to be on the lookout for us,' stated Drummond.

'Yeah, you could be right, Deadeye,' growled Wilton. 'So, Wyomin' it is.'

'But which town?' enquired Hank Pearson.

'Let's think about it. Medicine Bow an' Walcott are both flourishin' townships. I reckon each of their banks would be worth robbin'. An' they ain't much above a half-day's ride from here,' said Wilton.

'That's right. So, which is it to be?' demanded Drummond.

'Wa'al, I know a deserted huntin' lodge situated in the Medicine Bow Range, 'bout thirty miles from the town of the same name. We could set up camp there.'

'So, Medicine Bow's our target?'

'Yeah, Deadeye, I guess that's our best bet.' Wilton turned to Paul Springer. 'It'll be up to you to gauge whether a raid is feasible or not. If not, then you'll need to ride on to Walcott an' give that township the once-over.'

'Fine,' said Springer.

Blair Wilton washed down a last mouthful of taco with a gulp of coffee and clambered to his feet.

'OK. Let's git goin',' he rasped.

The others hastily finished eating and followed their chief out of the cantina.

Thereupon, they made for Providence Flat's

general store, where they purchased sufficient supplies in the form of food, drink and ammunition, to last them for the duration of their expedition. They also picked up half a dozen sticks of dynamite, as suggested by Paul Springer, together with an equal number of fulminate caps, a roll of sticky tape and a length of continuous fuse. From the store they went to the livery stables. And, a few minutes later, the six would-be bank robbers had saddled up and were heading out across the plain in the direction of the Medicine Bow Range.

It was evening by the time the Wilton gang reached the mountains. The hunting lodge was deserted, as Blair Wilton had said it would be. There were stables where the outlaws could house their horses. And, when they had tended to the animals' needs, they adjourned to the lodge, which consisted of one large communal room, a kitchen and half a dozen bedchambers. All the rooms were entirely devoid of furniture and, in consequence, the outlaws proposed to spend the night on the floor, with their saddles for pillows.

Firstly, however, they prepared supper. This consisted of hard tack, beef jerky and coffee, a somewhat less tasty meal than that which they had enjoyed at the cantina in Providence Flats. Nevertheless, it sufficed and, shortly afterwards, they settled down for the night. And, despite the hardness of the floor, all six, weary after their long ride, soon fell fast asleep.

They woke as dawn was breaking and, following a breakfast similar to their previous night's supper, Paul Springer made preparations for his departure. He was accompanied outside by Blair Wilton, who intended briefing his latest recruit prior to his setting out. And so, while Springer saddled his horse, the outlaw chief addressed him.

'You should reach Medicine Bow by late mornin',' he remarked.

'Yes.'

'That'll give you the rest of the day to acquaint yourself with the town. D'you figure that'll be long enough for you to size up the place?'

'I guess so.'

'Good! Then I can expect you back here sometime tomorrow. Unless you propose to return tonight?'

'I'd probably git lost in the dark. No, I'll spend the night in Medicine Bow an' set out at first light.'

'Yeah. That'll be time enough.'

'But s'pose I consider our chances of success in Medicine Bow to be kinda slim? Shall I instead head straight on to Walcott?'

'No.' Blair Wilton thought for a moment and said, 'If you do that, I won't know for sure that's why you ain't returned. No, you gotta report back here tomorrow.'

'But it's one helluva long ride an'. . . .'

'Wa'al, there's a way-station halfway between

Medicine Bow an' Walcott. Let's say I meet you there. Then, if you give Medicine Bow the thumbs up, we'll ride back to the lodge together an' make ready for our raid.'

'An' if I don't give Medicine Bow the thumbs up?'

'I come back here an' you ride on to Walcott an' give that town the once-over.'

'OK. That seems sensible.'

Blair Wilton smiled to himself. He thought it unlikely, but Paul Springer was new to the gang and there was always a chance that he might lose his nerve and abandon the venture. And Wilton had no wish to waste two or three days waiting at the hunting lodge for someone who was not intending to turn up. The rendezvous at the way-station would prevent any such delay occurring. Should Springer fail to put in an appearance on the morrow, Wilton would straightway return to the hunting lodge and formulate a fresh plan.

'Good luck,' he said. 'Until tomorrow.'

'Yeah,' said Springer. 'I'll be at the way-station by mid-mornin' at the latest.'

Whereupon, the man from Chicago mounted his horse and, with a cheery wave at the outlaw chief, set the animal cantering off in a north-easterly direction, down out of the foothills and towards the distant township of Medicine Bow.

# FOUR

It was shortly before noon when Doc Harris drove his covered wagon into Medicine Bow. Both on the canvas cover and on the side of the wagon itself was the legend: Dr Septimus Harris's Miracle Cure for All Ails. The doctor reined in the two horses that were hauling the wagon and came to a halt between the court house and Morris Broadfoot's funeral parlour. Thereupon, he stood up on the box and began to declaim.

A short, stocky figure in his mid-fifties, Doc Harris had a rosy, benevolent-looking countenance, a pair of twinkling blue eyes, snow-white hair and long, drooping whiskers of the same hue. He wore a white shirt and black bootlace tie, a long black coat and a tall, rather battered black stovepipe hat. He waved his arms about as he spoke and his declamations soon encouraged a small crowd to gather in the street around his wagon.

'Roll up, roll up, ladies and gentlemen, for the bargain of a lifetime. A wonder cure for all known ailments, namely croup, diarrhoea, influenza, pneumonia, consumption, a multitude of fevers, et cetera, et cetera. Yes, for only one dollar a bottle, I give you this miraculous brew, derived from a secret formula, which was conceived by none other than the great physician Hippocrates himself, and discovered by me while conducting lengthy researches in Athens, home of Greek philosophy and medicine.'

Among the crowd were the owner of a nearby horse ranch, Vince Clayton, and one of his wranglers. They were on their way to Sullivan's Saloon and had paused to listen to the medicine man's address.

Vince Clayton was a tall, lean man, born and bred in Wyoming. Forty years old, his serene grey eyes stared out from a craggy, weatherbeaten face, for Clayton was a man who was content with his lot in life. Married, with two young sons, he worked hard and long at his ranch, but it was work he enjoyed and the rewards, if not great, were sufficient for the wants of himself and his family. Attired in a black Stetson, check shirt, brown leather vest, denim pants and unspurred boots, he looked every inch the plainsman. His weapon, which he had never had recourse to use, was a Remington revolver carried in a holster on his right thigh.

His companion was an old army pal, who had volunteered to help out at the horse ranch after one of Clayton's two wranglers was thrown from a mustang and broke a leg. The army pal was in fact a legend in the West, namely the famous Kentuckian gunfighter, Jack Stone.

Six foot two inches in his stocking feet, Stone consisted of nigh on two hundred pounds of muscle and bone. He was pretty darned quick for a big man, though slow to anger. However, when riled, he displayed a ferocity which had earned him the name of being half mountain lion and half grizzly. The years had taken their toll, leaving scars, both mental and physical. The bullet holes had healed, but the broken nose remained and the emotional scars, which made Stone what he was, would never completely heal. His square-cut, deeply lined face had been handsome once and, now and again when he smiled, it regained something of its former good looks.

Someone had once said that Stone was a man born under a wandering star, yet this was not strictly true. It was through circumstances rather than inclination that Jack Stone had become a rover. Born the son of a Kentucky farmer, he most likely would still have been farming the family homesteading, had not his father been forced to sell it to pay off his gambling debts. Shortly afterwards, his father had been killed in a saloon brawl. Thereafter, the widow had struggled, alone and unaided, to bring up her young son. Stone was fourteen years old when, worn out by her efforts, she, too, had died. From that time onward, he had been on his own.

Stone had tried most things: farm work, ranch work, riding herd on several cattle drives, a little bronco-busting, even a spell working the gold mines of Colorado. Then, with the advent of the Civil War, he had fought for the Union and, afterwards for a while, served as an army scout. But the white man's savagery towards his red brother had sickened Stone and he had resigned.

Later, he had taken on a job as a ranch-hand in Nevada and met and married Mary Spencer, a local storekeeper's daughter. Once again, he had intended to sink roots. But it was not to be for, within a year, Mary died in childbirth, with the child stillborn. This tragic event had had a devastating effect on him, and it was some months before he recovered. He was, by then, a changed man: a man who would always be moving on, always looking for another frontier to cross.

His reputation as a gunfighter had been earned subsequently, with a series of jobs as stagecoach guard, deputy US marshal, deputy sheriff and, most famously, sheriff of Mallory, the roughest, toughest town in the State of Colorado. Indeed it was as the man who tamed Mallory that he became a legend of the West.

Now Jake Stone was looking for a quiet, peaceful life, and working for Vince Clayton on his horse ranch suited him perfectly. He followed the rancher into Sullivan's Saloon, a tall, broad-shouldered figure attired in grey Stetson, grey shirt, knee-length buckskin jacket, faded denim pants and unspurred boots. He wore a red kerchief round his strong, thick neck and on his right thigh he carried a Frontier Model Colt tied down.

'That there feller sure has the gift of the gab,' he chuckled, indicating, with a jerk of his thumb, the still declaiming Doc Harris.

'Yeah. Doubtless he'll kid a few trustin' folks into purchasin' his hogwash,' said Vince Clayton.

'You don't reckon it's as miraculous as he claims?'

'I sure don't. D'you?'

'Nope.'

Both men laughed and made their way across the bar-room to the counter, where Clayton ordered a couple of beers. The hot, dusty ride from the ranch to Medicine Bow had given them quite a thirst. They had ridden into town to pick up supplies. These they had obtained at the general store and piled onto Clayton's buckboard. Both the buckboard and Stone's bay gelding remained outside the store, which was situated on Main Street directly opposite the saloon. Their business concluded, the two men had determined to enjoy a few beers before setting off on their return journey.

There was a fair crowd in the saloon and both its bartenders were being kept busy. The proprietor, Art Sullivan, was keeping a careful eye on the proceedings and was ready, if need be, to slip behind the bar and help his staff. However, at present they were coping quite well and, therefore, he was free to remain on the customers' side, where he was deep in conversation with Marshal Joe Paine, Medicine Bow's mayor, the hotelier Sidney Greenridge and its deputy mayor, the lawyer Richard Thomas.

All four men were similarly dressed, in three-piece, city-style suits. And all except the marshal wore Derby hats. He sported a black, low-crowned Stetson and his badge of office was pinned to the front of his jacket.

Both the saloonkeeper and the marshal were large, jolly men, with florid complexions, while the mayor was short, fat and pompous-looking, and his deputy tall and thin, with a pale, somewhat lugubrious countenance.

' 'Mornin', Vince, Jack,' Art Sullivan greeted the rancher and the Kentuckian.

' 'Mornin', fellers,' responded Vince Clayton, while Jack Stone merely smiled and raised his glass in salutation.

'You seen that mountebank 'tween the court house an' Morris Broadfoot's place?' enquired the mayor.

'Seems he's offerin' folks the elixir of life,' laughed Sullivan.

'Hogwash, that's all it is,' declared Clayton, repeating what he had said earlier to Stone.

'Reckon so,' agreed Marshal Joe Paine.

'Nevertheless, I'll wager he sells plenty of it,' said Richard Thomas.

'Ah, but is it legal so to do, Richard? If he's doin' so by falsely claimin' it has attributes that it most certainly doesn't have. . . .' began Sidney Greenridge.

'You askin' me to run him outa town, Mr Mayor?' enquired Joe Paine.

'Wa'al. . . .'

'That'd be a mite drastic,' interjected Clayton. 'I say let the feller ply his dubious trade. If folks is dumb enough to buy his so-called medicine, let 'em. I don't expect it'll do 'em any harm.'

'H'mm, I s'pose not,' concurred the mayor, albeit a trifle reluctantly.

'An' he sure is entertainin',' added Stone.

'Yes. I'll give him that,' said Greenridge.

There was further discussion of Doc Harris's fantastic claims and it was while this was still in full flow that Paul Springer rode into town. The man from Chicago proceeded slowly down Main Street and dismounted outside Sullivan's Saloon. He hitched his horse to the rail, but, before entering the saloon, he strolled over to join the crowd listening to Doc Harris. By this time, the good doctor's elixir was much in demand and he was busy selling bottles of it to gullible townsfolk. The purchasers were, in the main, ladies of a certain age whose ailments were mostly imaginary.

Paul Springer watched the performance with interest, for he recognized the man. He, Springer, had fled Chicago on being caught *in flagrante delicto* with the mistress of the gangster, Big Tony Demarco. Well, the supposed doctor had been an integral member of Big Tony's gang. So what on earth, wondered Springer, had caused him to head out West under the assumed name of Dr Septimus Harris? Springer had known him as Keith 'Fingers' Muldoon. He grinned and called out, ' 'Mornin', Fingers. Fancy bumpin' into you way out here!'

Doc Harris started and almost dropped a bottle of his precious brew. Then, when he saw who had hailed him by his pseudonym, he relaxed, for he recalled only too well the incident that had prompted Paul Springer to leave Chicago in such a hurry. Springer was definitely in no position to denounce him.

'I'd prefer it if you would address me by my proper title,' he rasped.

Springer continued to grin.

'As you please, Doc,' he replied, doffing his hat, and then turning, he headed back towards Sullivan's Saloon.

Doc Harris resumed his sales pitch and continued dispensing bottles of his *Miracle Cure for All Ails* to an eager public. Of those gathered before the doctor's wagon only Deputy Marshal Ted Hume had noted, and was puzzled by, Dr Septimus Harris being addressed as Fingus rather than Septimus. He had slightly misheard Paul Springer and, after some cogitation, assumed that perhaps the doctor had two Christian names, one of which he had omitted from his advertisement for the sake of brevity.

Ted Hume was about the same age as the marshal, a stocky, bald-headed individual, of little or no ambition, yet a loyal and reliable lieutenant. Joe Paine's other deputy, Chuck Finn, was, in contrast, an energetic young fellow, dark-haired and slim-built. He was fairly new at the job and had high hopes of one day succeeding Paine as marshal of Medicine Bow. He was minding the law office while Hume patrolled the streets and his superior enjoyed a few lunchtime beers in the saloon, as the marshal did most days in company with the mayor and *his* deputy.

Paul Springer, having succeeded in startling Doc Harris, was now anxious to proceed with his commission. On the ride from the hunting lodge to

Medicine Bow he had formed a plan of campaign. He would check out the town, taking particular note of the law office's proximity to the bank. Then, posing as a real estate agent, he would attempt to make the mayor's acquaintance and, through him, that of the bank manager. He had completed the first part of his plan, ascertaining that the law office was situated next door to the Cattlemen's Bank and immediately opposite the Medicine Bow Hotel. He had passed all three on his way into town, and it was now time to proceed with part two of the plan.

As Springer stepped up on to the sidewalk in front of the saloon, he chanced to glance down Main Street and observe the spire of Medicine Bow's small wooden church spearing up into the sky. The sight of the church gave Springer an idea. He did a quick calculation. He and the Wilton gang had left Providence Flats on Thursday and he was due to rendezvous with Blair Wilton on the morrow, Saturday. Springer grinned wickedly. He had been less than happy upon discovering that the bank and the law office were adjacent, but now he did not care. His newly-formed plan would surely take care of that little problem.

Springer pushed open the batwing doors and strolled into Sullivan's Saloon. He figured that he would find someone in the saloon to direct him to the mayor's office and, anyway, he was sorely in need of a cool, refreshing beer.

He approached the bar close to where Art Sullivan was deep in conversation with the marshal, the mayor and the others. Observing the marshal's badge pinned to his jacket, Springer decided to broach him. So, having purchased and tasted his beer, he waited until there was a lull in the conversation. Then he promptly addressed the law officer.

'Excuse me buttin' in, Marshal,' he said.

'Yes?' Marshal Joe Paine eyed the newcomer curiously. 'What can I do for you?' he asked.

'I'm a stranger in town an' I'm lookin' to find the mayor,' explained Springer.

'You're in luck, then,' said Paine, 'for this here's our mayor, Mr Sidney Greenridge.'

'That's me,' said the little man, puffing out his chest and smiling smugly.

'Pleased to meet you, Mr Greenridge.' Springer extended his hand and declared, 'I'm Paul Jones, an' I represent Chicago Premier Real Estate Inc.'

'Indeed?'

'Yes. An' I have a proposition to put to you,' said Springer. 'But, first of all, let me buy you an' your friends a drink.'

Greenridge positively beamed.

'That's mighty civil of you,' he replied and proceeded to introduce Springer to the others in the group.

All except Greenridge asked for beer. He opted for whiskey, a fine Tennessee blend, reserved by Art Sullivan for himself and only a few select customers. Then, when they had toasted each other, Greenridge enquired, 'OK, Mr Jones, what's this proposition you're wantin' to put to me?'

Paul Springer smiled silkily.

'Wa'al, Mr Mayor, it's like this: Chicago Premier Real Estate Inc. is interested in purchasin' tracts of land which it deems could be used for development purposes. There are many townships across the length an' breadth of the United States that are ripe for expansion an', indeed, are expandin'. Fast. Medicine Bow could be one such township, an' I am here to assess the situation.'

'Should you conclude that our town is, as you put it, ripe for expansion, an' you report this fact back to your company, what then?' asked Greenridge.

'Chicago Premier Real Estate Inc. has the money to purchase the land an' promote the town's development.' Springer glanced from the mayor to his deputy and continued: 'In these circumstances, everyone would benefit: those from whom we bought the land, the various local businesses and tradesmen an' the community in general. In truth, the result would be an expandin' an' thrivin' economy.'

'Would you have need of a local lawyer?' asked Richard Thomas, his normally lugubrious features showing some unaccustomed animation.

'Our worthy deputy mayor practises the law,' explained Joe Paine, with a grin. Springer smiled broadly at the lawyer.

'Of course,' he said. 'We should want you to help negotiate with those landowners whose property we were interested in acquirin'. Your legal advice would be indispensable.'

Now it was the turn of Sidney Greenridge to appear animated, for he owned much of the land immediately surrounding the town.

'You can rely upon me an' Mr Thomas to assist you in any way we can,' he declared. 'After all, as mayor an' deppity mayor, we naturally have the best interests of Medicine Bow at heart.'

'Naturally,' concurred Thomas. 'So, if there is anythin' we can do to facilitate. . . .'

'A guided tour of the town would be a help,' said Springer.

'I shall personally undertake to show you round,' said the mayor.

'Thank you.'

'It will be my pleasure.'

'An', should you have anythin' of a legal nature, which you wish to discuss . . .' began Thomas.

'We shall be sure to drop into your office,' said Greenridge.

'Yes.' Springer finished his beer and turned to the

mayor. 'Wa'al, Mr Mayor, shall we be goin'? I should like to conclude my survey today an' leave tomorrow at first light.'

'So soon?' said Greenridge.

'Wa'al, y'see, I have other towns to survey. An' the sooner I complete those surveys an' submit my reports, the sooner Chicago Premier Real Estate Inc. can come to a decision an' git things movin'.'

'S'pose you give Medicine Bow a good report, yet your company still decides against developin' the town, will they let us know?' demanded Thomas.

'I think that's highly unlikely to be the case. If I recommend a town for development, you can rest assured that Chicago Premier Real Estate Inc. will invest in that development. However, whatever the decision, I promise we'll let you know.'

'How long. . . ?'

'A few weeks, I'm afraid, Mr Thomas, although I intend to conduct the surveys with all possible dispatch.'

'To which end, let your guided tour begin,' said Greenridge.

He ushered Springer across the bar-room and out of the saloon, closely followed by his deputy.

While Richard Thomas returned to his office, where he had business to attend, the mayor proceeded to escort Paul Springer round the town. As it consisted of Main Street and merely a couple of very short streets intersecting this thoroughfare, one named North and the other South Street, the tour did not take too long to complete. Springer, however, in his assumed role of land developer, asked a plethora of questions and carefully studied the principal buildings, namely the court house, the town hall, the town's sole hotel, the livery stables and, last but not least, the bank.

'An' now,' declared Springer, at the end of their walk, 'I should like to circumambulate Medicine Bow, for it is the land immediately surrounding it that we shall require for development.'

'Of course,' said Greenridge.

The second tour took slightly longer than the first, for the fat little mayor was unused to walking far and, following their earlier perambulation, his pace slackened considerably. Springer pretended not to notice the other's evident fatigue and continued to ply him with questions regarding the ownership of the land over which they were tramping. Greenridge was only too pleased to tell Springer that most of it was in his, Greenridge's possession. And so, when they returned for a second time to the front of Sullivan's Saloon, it was a weary, but jubilant mayor who suggested they repair inside for further discussion and refreshment.

This time, hot and flustered, Sidney Greenridge opted for a long, cool beer, as did an equally thirsty Paul Springer. They adjourned to a corner table, where the mayor asked eagerly, 'Wa'al, Mr Jones, whaddya think? Is Medicine Bow ripe for development?'

'I b'lieve it is, Mr Greenridge, and I shall say as much when I report back,' replied Springer, smiling silkily.

'Splendid!' exclaimed the delighted mayor.

' 'Course if we go ahead, we shall have to transfer a great deal of money to the bank here in town, to pay the various contractors an' tradesfolk who will necessarily be involved in the expansion.'

'Naturally.'

'You have jest the one bank, I note.'

'That's right. The Cattlemen's Bank. A solid, well-established bank, with branches throughout Wyomin' an', indeed, the entire West.'

'I should like to visit your branch, jest to assure myself that it is a safe repository for the vast amount of money which Chicago Premier Real Estate Inc. would be likely to deposit.'

'Of course, Mr Jones. Let me escort you there an' introduce you to the manager, Mr Hamilton Scott.'

'A good Scotch name.'

'Yes. Hamilton's a shrewd, hard-headed Scot.' Greenridge threw back the remains of his beer and declared, 'Come, let's go meet him.'

Springer finished his drink and followed the mayor out of the saloon. Two minutes later, they entered the bank. It was pretty crowded, with a small queue formed in front of each of the three tellers. As they served their customers, sitting on their high stools, the manager remained in his office, busily engaged in his administrative duties, yet cocking an eye in their direction from time to time. Thus it was that he observed the mayor and his companion enter the premises. Immediately, he rose and stepped out of the office. He raised the flap in the counter, which separated the bank staff from their customers, and beckoned the two men to come through to his side of it.

'Howdy-do, Sidney. Is this call on business or pleasure?' he enquired of the mayor.

'Both, I hope,' replied Greenridge. 'Allow me to introduce you to Mr Paul Jones. Mr Jones, this here's Mr Hamilton Scott.'

The pair shook hands and then Hamilton Scott ushered the visitors into his office and shut the door.

'Business is brisk today, Hamilton,' commented the mayor, as he and Springer seated themselves upon the chairs offered to them.

'It sure is. But, then, we're always pretty darned busy,' stated Scott. He retreated behind his desk and sat down. 'Well, Sidney, what can I do for you?' he asked.

'It's not what you can do for me, Hamilton. It's what you can do for Mr Jones here,' remarked Greenridge.

Hamilton Scott cast a speculative eye at Paul Springer.

'Indeed? And just what is it that I can do for you?' he asked.

Springer smiled and explained his supposed business in Medicine Bow. He concluded by saying, 'Naturally, my company will need to transfer a great deal of money to the town. As I was explaining to Mr Greenridge—'

'Of course! Of course!' Scott interrupted him. 'I quite see that. And you have come along to the bank to satisfy yourself that your company's money could be safely deposited here?'

'Exactly.'

'Well, situated as we are next door to the law office, this branch could not be better placed.'

'Provided that the law office is manned twenty-four hours a day.'

'It is. Marshal Paine and his two deputies ensure that there is always one or other of them on the premises.'

'Even overnight?'

'Yes. Their nightshifts are organized on a rota basis.'

'What about the Sabbath? I observed you have a church on the edge of town. Surely, your peace officers will wish to attend the Sunday services?'

'Sunday duties are also performed on a strict rota.

One Sunday in three.'

'Hmm. Wa'al, Mr Scott, that seems entirely satisfactory,' conceded Springer. 'However, I also must ask you about your security arrangements.'

'There are two doors. One at the front of the bank, through which our customers may enter. And one at the rear, through which myself and my staff come and go. Both are locked at night and I am the sole keyholder.'

'That, too, seems entirely satisfactory.' Springer smiled genially and, glancing at the huge iron safe which occupied one corner of the bank manager's small office, remarked, 'That is certainly a splendid looking safe. I see that it has a combination lock.'

'Yes.'

'An' do you have the combination, Mr Scott?'

'I do.'

'An' does anyone else?'

'No.'

'You keep a record of it somewhere?'

'Yes.' Hamilton Scott tapped his head. 'In here,' he said.

'It is not written down anywhere?'

'No.'

'But what if, Heaven forbid, something happened to you, an accident or. . . ?' Springer left the rest of his question unsaid.

'In that unlikely event,' said Scott, 'my chief teller

would immediately telegraph the bank's headquarters in Chicago, and someone would be dispatched to Medicine Bow with the appropriate combination.'

'Hmm. In the meantime, that could prove rather inconvenient for the bank's customers.'

'Yes; but, as I said, it's unlikely to happen and, even if it did, the train journey from Chicago to Medicine Bow takes only about twenty hours. Less than one day.'

Springer nodded his head. He then produced a small black leather case, inside of which were half a dozen fine Havana cigars. He offered them to the mayor and the bank manager and took one himself. Then, when all three were lit, he said quietly, 'My report to Chicago Premier Real Estate Inc. will be favourable in all respects.'

Sidney Greenridge puffed out his chest and grinned delightedly, while Hamilton Scott's thin, austere features almost broke into a smile.

Thus was their business concluded. Thereafter, Greenridge insisted on escorting Springer to the Medicine Bow Hotel, where he installed him in its finest room at no charge.

'That's mighty generous of you, Mr Greenridge,' exclaimed Springer.

'Not at all. An' this evenin' you must come dine with me an' my wife. Ours is the first house you come to on North Street. You cain't miss it. It's the only

74

two-storey residence in the street,' he explained proudly.

'Ah, so you don't reside in the hotel!' said Springer.

'No. I leave that in the care of a manager, Seth Burroughs; a good man.' Greenridge smiled and continued, 'I have a variety of business interests an', of course, my civic duties, which take up much of my time.'

'You must be a very busy man,' remarked Springer.

'Oh, I am; I am!' declared the mayor. 'Anyways, make yourself at home here. Anythin' you want is on the house. Jest ask Seth. An' I'll look forward to seein' you this evenin' at seven o' clock. In the meantime, I have both those business interests an' my civic duties to attend to.'

'Until this evenin', Mr Mayor.'

'Until then, Mr Jones.'

Paul Springer took off his jacket and shoes and stretched out on the hotel bed. He puffed on his cigar and smiled to himself. Everything was working out perfectly. The plan he had devised was foolproof. He was looking forward to expounding it to Blair Wilton when they met at the way-station on the following morning.

# FIVE

It was past midnight when Paul Springer left the mayor's house in North Street. He had spent a most convivial evening with Sidney Greenridge and his wife, Sally. They had eaten well and he and the mayor had consumed a copious quantity of Greenridge's fine old Tennessee whiskey. Consequently, both men were in high spirits when they parted.

'Like I said, I shall be off at first light,' said Springer. 'But you can be sure I'll let you know, jest as soon as my various surveys are complete an' a decision has been made, as to where Chicago Premier Real Estate Inc. intends to invest its money.'

'You consider, though, that Medicine Bow is ripe for development?' said Greenridge eagerly.

'I do. The company may well decide to back several different developments, an', at this stage, I cannot say which. Nevertheless, I am pretty confident that the development of this town will be one of them,' replied Springer.

Greenridge beamed, as he contemplated the vast amount of money he would undoubtedly get should Springer's company go ahead with the project.

'Splendid!' he boomed and thrust out his hand.

The two men shook hands. Then Greenridge retreated indoors, while Springer set off along Main Street towards his hotel. As he turned out of North Street, he glanced at the long, rectangular one-storey building standing on the left-hand corner between it and the town's main thoroughfare. He smiled inwardly, running his eye over the silent bank. A shaft of yellow light streamed out of the front window of the adjacent law office. Which particular peace officer was on duty tonight, he wondered?

As he carried on, Springer observed, that, further on down Main Street, Sullivan's Saloon remained open and, beyond the saloon, Doc Harris's covered wagon still stood between the court house and Morris Broadfoot's funeral parlour. He turned to cross the street towards the Medicine Bow Hotel when suddenly he was struck by an idea. Was it an inspiration or simply a foolish thought not worth pursuing? He stood for a few moments, mulling over the matter in his mind. And, the longer he thought about it, the more the idea appealed to him. Therefore, without more ado, he changed direction and headed down the sidewalk towards the covered wagon.

The wagon lay in darkness. It was evident that Doc Harris had retired for the night. Springer did not hesitate. He clambered up on to the box and, thrusting his head inside the wagon, yelled, 'Fingers! Wake up!'

He had to repeat himself no fewer than three times before a bleary-eyed Doc Harris started up and hastily lit the lantern which hung above his head.

So dim was the light and so dulled by sleep was Doc Harris's brain that it took him some moments before he recognized Paul Springer.

'Goddammit, what the hell are you doin' in my wagon?' he exclaimed. 'An', 'sides, I thought I told you to address me by my proper title!'

'Proper title be damned,' retorted Springer. 'You ain't no more a doctor than I am.'

'Now listen here—'

'No; you listen here, Mr Keith Muldoon, better known as Fingers. I've got a proposition I wanta put to you.'

'OK! OK! But jest stop callin' me Fingers.'

'Very well, *Doc.* You prepared to listen to what I've gotta say?'

'Yeah, I s'pose.' Muldoon, alias Doc Harris, sounded less than enthusiastic.

'Wa'al, before I begin, mebbe you'll tell me what you're doin' here masqueradin' as some quack doctor?'

78

'I had to leave Chicago in a hurry. Kinda like you did.'

Springer grinned.

'You ain't tellin' me that you was caught tumblin' Big Tony's mistress, too?' he remarked.

Muldoon shook his head.

'No, nuthin' like that,' he said.

'Then, what. . . ?'

'Shortly after you skipped town, the Chicago city police, led by that Scotch sonofabitch, Allan Pinkerton, arrested Big Tony.'

'On what charge?'

'Murder. Dutch Olafsen was tryin' to muscle in on Big Tony's territory.'

'Not a wise move.'

'No. So, Big Tony topped him. Personally. Unfortunately, there were witnesses, me included. I don't know 'bout the others, but I thought it best to leave town.' Fingers Muldoon shuddered and explained, 'I don't reckon none of them witnesses is likely to live long enough to testify.'

'Surely the police will protect 'em?'

'They'll try. But. . . .' Muldoon shrugged his shoulders. 'I wasn't prepared to chance it. I took the first train outa town, 'fore Pinkerton's men could git hold of me.'

'An' set yourself up as a purveyor of a *Miracle Cure for All Ails.*'

'Yeah. It took every last cent I had. But it's paid off. I'm makin' a decent livin' sellin' my potions.'

'You aimin' to do that for the rest of your life?'

'Hell, no! I figure on workin' my way across to the western seaboard an' settlin' in 'Frisco. Under another name, of course.'

'Of course.'

'I hear 'Frisco's the kinda place a man could make hisself a fortune.'

'So, are you thinkin' of takin' up your old profession?'

'No, I ain't. I'm stayin' legit.'

'You call sellin' that dodgy medicine legit?'

'It ain't against the law.'

'No, I'll grant you that. So, whaddya reckon on doin' when you finally reach 'Frisco?'

'Mebbe open a saloon, or a dance hall, or a gamblin' joint? Some place where I can earn real big bucks.'

'You'll need a considerable amount of capital to start up any of those enterprises. D'you reckon you'll have accumulated sufficient by the time you reach 'Frisco?'

Muldoon shrugged his shoulders. He lived in the hope that he might, yet he realized it was quite likely he wouldn't.

'Mebbe not,' he admitted ruefully.

Paul Springer smiled.

'Then, will you listen to my proposition?' he asked.

'Oh, why not? Go on, spit it out,' said Muldoon.

'Wa'al, this is what I propose,' said Springer, and he went on to inform Muldoon of his alliance with Blair Wilton and his gang, of their plan to rob the Cattlemen's Bank and of the change of plan that had suddenly occurred to him upon spotting Muldoon's wagon. 'So, whaddya think?' he enquired.

Muldoon gave the matter some thought. And, like Springer before him, the longer he thought about it, the more the idea appealed to him. He was confident that he could easily perform the task Springer had in mind for him, and, moreover, he felt sure the plan would work. His attitude towards his late-night visitor had changed radically. He rose and grasped the other warmly by the hand.

'I'm your man,' he said fervently.

The two men shook hands.

'Until the allotted hour,' said Springer.

'I'll be there,' affirmed Muldoon.

Springer climbed out of the wagon and, leaving his soon-to-be accomplice to return to his bed, he crossed the street and headed towards his hotel.

He slept but fitfully that night and got up as dawn was breaking. Anxious to be on his way, Springer forewent breakfast and immediately rode off, out of town and in the direction of the way-station where he had agreed to rendezvous with Blair Wilton. Before he left town, however, he passed the church and read the noticeboard outside. It gave the name of the minister and the times of its various services, The main Sunday morning service was scheduled to take place at ten a.m.

The way-station was situated on the main east-west trail some eight miles west of Medicine Bow. It consisted of a general store-cum-bar-room, together with a rickety barn, three tumbledown stables and a small corral. The way-station was run by a short, fat half-breed named Panama Pete. A pair of shifty black eyes, a pug nose, a drooping black moustache and a wide mouth, forever smiling and displaying a full set of dazzling white teeth, were evident beneath the battered sombrero which Panama Pete wore at all times, both indoors and out. His dark-blue cotton shirt and black cotton trousers were partially covered by a rather grubby white apron. He presided behind a large wooden counter, surrounded by all manner of goods: sacks of coffee, beef jerky, hard tack, piles of blankets, various rifles and handguns, ammunition, bottles of red-eye; in fact, almost everything a traveller might need. In front of the counter was a scattering of tables and chairs, where a man could sit and quench his thirst with a long, cold beer. However, no such customers were in evidence when Paul Springer entered. He was Panama Pete's first customer of the day.

'*Buenos días, señor,*' Panama Pete greeted him with an ingratiating smile. 'How may I be of service to you?'

'Pork 'n' beans, cornbread an' a cuppa coffee,' retorted Springer briskly.

'Of course, *señor*. Please to take a seat.'

Springer nodded, and went across and sat down at one of the dozen or so tables. Panama Pete, meanwhile, retreated a few steps and directed a torrent of Spanish towards the rear quarters of the store. Then he smiled again at Springer and explained, 'My wife, she will bring you your breakfast *pronto.*'

And, sure enough, a few minutes later his wife appeared bearing a large plateful of pork and beans and a jug of coffee. She placed these items down before Springer and then fetched him a knife, a fork, a mug and a basket containing several thick slices of bread.

'I wish you a good appetite, *señor,*' she said, as she turned and headed back to her quarters.

Paul Springer set to work with a will. The early morning ride from Medicine Bow had made him very hungry. Consequently, he wolfed down the food in next to no time. Thereafter, he lingered over his coffee and, indeed, ordered a second jug.

By the time Springer had consumed the second jug of coffee, a few other travellers had entered the way-station. A couple of itinerant cowboys were breakfasting at an adjacent table, a whiskey salesman was attempting to press his wares upon Panama Pete and a buffalo hunter had called to purchase a bag of coffee and some ammunition.

It was mid-morning, however, before Blair Wilton eventually arrived. By this time Springer had progressed from coffee to beer. He rose and greeted the outlaw chief. Then he fetched Wilton a beer and replenished his own glass.

'Success to our enterprise!' he proposed, raising his glass and taking a large draught of the amber liquid.

Blair Wilton grinned and glanced quickly round the tables. The two itinerant cowboys had departed some time earlier. The whiskey salesman had concluded his business with Panama Pete and also departed. Only the buffalo hunter remained. He sat with his purchases, at a table near the counter, and was busily demolishing a gargantuan meal of steak, eggs, spicy sausage, beans and cornbread. Blair Wilton lowered his voice to ensure that the man remained out of earshot.

'OK, give it to me,' he rasped. 'D'you reckon we can take the Medicine Bow bank?'

'I do,' replied Springer. 'Providin' we delay the raid till tomorrow.'

'Why wait? If—'

'Tomorrow is Sunday.'

'So?'

'Like in most cattle towns, the bank is situated next to the law office. Which ain't good news. But again, like in most cattle towns, its church or chapel is situated on the edge of town. Which is good news.'

'In which way?'

'On the Sabbath most of the population will be attendin' church, includin' two of the town's three peace officers. It seems they work to a rota.'

'So, we jest ride into town an'—'

'No.'

'No?' Blair Wilton's rugged features contorted into a puzzled frown.

'Let me explain. A short side street bisects Main Street north to south. If you were to ride straight across the plain, approachin' the town from the north an' passin' behind the houses which line the east side of North Street, you would almost certainly reach the rear of the bank unobserved. Now the bank is on the left-hand corner of North Street and Main Street and is a long, rectangular one-storey building. It has two doors, one at the front for the admittance of its customers and another at the back for the admittance of its staff. Got the picture?'

The puzzled frown left Blair Wilton's face, to be replaced by a wicked grin.

'I reckon Gil Ambrose'd easily pick the lock an' let us in,' he stated.

'Unfortunately, the safe has a combination lock. I don't s'pose Gil would be up to crackin' that open?' said Springer.

'No. Like we said a coupla days back, that would take a real cracksman.'

'So, you will need to use a few sticks of that dynamite we bought. The resultin' explosion will undoubtedly alert the population. But, for the most part, they'll be in church on the edge of town. Therefore, by the time they recover from the shock, scramble outa church an' reach the bank, you an' the gang should have stuffed your saddlebags full of banknotes an' be well on your way. Doubtless, the marshal will try to form a posse, but that'll take time. I don't figure they will have a cat in hell's chance of catchin' up with you.'

Blair Wilton leant forward and clapped Springer on the shoulder.

'You've done well,' he declared delightedly. 'The only feller likely to reach the bank 'fore we lam outa there is the duty peace officer. An' I'll set Deadeye to gun him down soon as he sticks his head outa his office.'

'You'll adopt my plan, then?' said Springer.

'Sure will. So, what time do we hit the bank tomorrow?'

'Sometime durin' the church service, which commences at ten a.m.'

' 'Bout ten minutes past ten should be jest right.'

'Yeah.'

'Wa'al, let's have another beer an' then head back to the huntin' lodge,' suggested Wilton.

'You head back there, Blair. Me, I intend returnin' to Medicine Bow,' replied Springer.

The outlaw chief stared at him, a look of incredulity on his face.

'You ain't joinin' us on the raid?' he gasped.

'No.'

'But. . . .'

'This could be the first of several bank raids, right?'

'Er . . . yeah, I guess so.'

'In which case, you'd need me to reconnoitre each time.'

'Sure.'

'Then it's imperative that no suspicion should fall upon me.' Springer smiled and explained how he had taken in the mayor, the deputy mayor and the bank manager, and would want to use the same ploy in the future. 'So, you see,' he concluded, 'I must return to Medicine Bow, havin' supposedly carried out further surveys. Then, tomorrow, I propose to attend their church service an', afterwards, join any posse that is formed.'

'Wa'al, I dunno.'

'If I don't do this, an' they *do* connect me with the

bank robbery, my description an' my mode of operation will be circulated to every goddam law office in Wyomin'. This is the age of the telegraph, remember.'

Blair Wilton nodded. If this was to be the first of many such raids, what Paul Springer proposed made good sense.

'What about your share of the loot?' he enquired. 'Ain't you afraid me an' the boys might jest share it between us an' then split up?'

'I'll take that chance,' said Springer. 'I don't see you passin' up the opportunity to strike again, an' again, an' again. One successful raid ain't gonna make you all rich. Several might jest do that.'

'Yeah.' Wilton smiled broadly at this thought. 'So, whereabouts d'you reckon we should rendezvous?' he asked.

'Back at the huntin' lodge?'

'No. I don't figure we'll head back there after the raid. It's too darned near to Medicine Bow. Those out lookin' for us might stumble across it.'

'Then where?'

'Providence Flats. We'll be safer there.'

Paul Springer made out that he was considering this suggestion.

'OK,' he said presently. 'You an' the rest of the boys wait for me there. I'll leave town as soon as I think it's politic to do so, but it could be a coupla days or more 'fore I reach Providence Flats.'

'That's OK.'

Blair Wilton purchased two more beers and, when they had drunk them, the pair rose and headed for the door. The half-breed wished them *buenos días* as they left, while the buffalo hunter didn't even bother to look up from his meal.

Outside, they shook hands, mounted their horses and parted. Blair Wilton headed back towards the mountains and the hunting lodge. Paul Springer took the main trail east in the direction of Medicine Bow. However, he did not ride directly into town. Two miles short of Medicine Bow, he turned off the trail and into a stand of cottonwoods.

A small stream ran through the wood. Springer made camp beside this, out of sight of anyone who might happen to pass along the trail. He unsaddled his horse and, sitting with his back to a tree, lit up a cheroot and settled down. He had a long wait ahead of him.

# SIX

A scorching hot August sun beat down on that Sunday morning as the citizens of Medicine Bow flocked to church. Among the first to arrive were Vince Clayton and his family riding on a buckboard and, alongside, Jack Stone on his bay gelding. Various other ranchers and homesteaders, together with their families, drove or rode up to the church at about the same time or shortly afterwards. All of them had several miles to travel and, therefore, had set out early. The townsfolk, on the other hand, were all living within a few hundred yards of the church and most tended to leave home as late as possible, arriving within a few minutes of the commencement of the service.

Exceptions to this rule were Hamilton Scott the bank manager, Marshal Joe Paine and his family, and deputy mayor Richard Thomas and his family. They invariably arrived in good time, while the mayor and his wife did not. Sidney and Sally Greenridge deliberately came at the last moment, for both liked to make a grand entry.

On that particular Sunday the Greenridges arrived at the church with barely a minute to spare. Nevertheless, they proceeded at a stately gait down the aisle towards their seats in one of the two front pews. As they did so, they acknowledged the presence of a select few of Medicine Bow's dignitaries with either a smile or a nod of the head. Finally, they sat down next to Richard Thomas, his wife and children and immediately in front of Marshal Joe Paine. The marshal and his family were sharing their pew with one of his two deputies, Ted Hume. It was the turn of the other, younger deputy, Chuck Finn, to man the law office that morning.

No sooner had Sidney and Sally Greenridge settled in their pew than they were obliged to rise as the choir, closely followed by the verger and the pastor, entered through a side door to the strains of the hymn, *All Things Bright And Beautiful.* In the absence of an organ, this was played upon a piano. The choir, consisting mainly of elderly women, sang the hymn with brio, while the congregation joined in lustily, if not altogether tunefully.

As the hymn rang out across the deserted town, Blair Wilton and his gang rode towards it across the plain. They followed Paul Springer's instructions to the letter and drew up behind the long, low building that was the Cattlemen's Bank. Then they promptly dismounted.

Blair Wilton glanced anxiously at the rear door of the law office, fearful that the thunder of their horses' hoofs might have alerted whoever was within. But he need not have worried. Chuck Finn had consumed rather too many beers the night before and was fast asleep in the marshal's armchair, his feet resting on the desk in front of him.

'OK, boys, let's git to it,' rasped Wilton. 'Grab your saddlebags. You're gonna be stuffin' 'em full of banknotes.' He turned to Deadeye Drummond. 'But not you, Deadeye. You take care of the hosses. An' keep a weather eye open for the duty peace officer. When the safe blows, he'll be sure to come runnin'.'

Deadeye Drummond's weaselly features split into an evil grin.

'You can rely on me, Blair. Soon as he pops his head outa his office, I'll plug the sonofabitch.'

Wilton nodded and turned to Gil Ambrose.

'Gil, you jest gonna stand there, or are you gonna pick the goddam lock?' he demanded.

The fat Easterner smiled nervously.

'I . . . I was about to . . . to s . . . start on it,' he stammered.

'Wa'al, git on with it,' snarled Wilton.

Gil Ambrose nodded and hurriedly approached the bank's back door. To his relief, he found the lock easy to pick. Indeed, he had picked dozens of similar locks in his time. He pushed the door open and the outlaws piled inside. They quickly found the huge iron safe in a corner of the bank manager's office. Wilton eyed the combination lock.

'I don't s'pose you could pick that there lock?' he enquired of Gil Ambrose.

Ambrose shook his head.

'No,' he said. 'I can pick most door-locks, but that . . . that's a job for a real cracksman.'

Wilton would have been surprised had Ambrose said otherwise, but he had felt he should ask before resorting to the dynamite. Now he began to empty the small canvas bag which, together with his saddle-bags, he had brought into the bank. It contained all the equipment he needed to blow open the safe.

The outlaw chief cautiously opened the canvas bag and extracted in succession six sticks of dynamite, some fulminate caps, a roll of sticky tape and a length of fuse. Hank Pearson eyed the sticks of dynamite and muttered, 'You ain't aimin' to use all six of them sticks, are yuh?'

'No, I guess not. I ain't done this before, so. . . .' began Wilton.

'Two sticks should suffice,' interjected Gil Ambrose.

'Oh, yeah?' snarled Wilton.

'Yeah. I was present once when some friends of mine blew a safe. Back in Boston, Massachusetts. A coupla sticks did the job.'

'OK. Two sticks it is, then.'

Wilton carefully replaced four sticks in the canvas bag. The other two he carried across to the safe. He stared at the huge iron box. Would they be sufficient to blast it open? He would soon find out.

Handling the sticks, while he attached the fulminate caps and then fixed them to the door of the safe with sticky tape, was not something Wilton did lightly. Although not of a nervous disposition, the outlaw was not used to dealing with explosives and, by the time they were securely attached to the safe, he was perspiring copiously.

He paused for a few moments to regain his composure. Then he wiped his brow, grinned at his accomplices and began to lay out the length of fuse. It stretched through the manager's office, across the space behind the counter where the tellers worked, and into that part of the bank where the customers wait. He drew it round the counter to a point almost directly opposite the safe.

'OK, boys,' he said, 'you'd best join me on this side of the counter. Frank, you take that bag containin' the rest of them sticks of dynamite an' leave it outside.'

'Sure thing, Blair.'

Frank Pearson picked up the canvas bag and did as he was bid. Then he re-entered the bank and joined his cousin and Gil Ambrose, who were, by now, crouching down beside their chief.

Blair Wilton felt in the pocket of his Prince Albert coat and withdrew a packet of lucifers. He struck a light at the first attempt and immediately the fuse began to burn. Wilton watched it burn its way across the floor and fizz off round the counter.

The outlaws crouched there in silence, their hands clapped over their ears. The seconds ticked by. The wait seemed interminable. Wilton began to look worried. He glanced quizzically at Gil Ambrose.

'D'you think the fuse has burned itself out?' he whispered.

Ambrose opened his mouth to reply, but, before he could speak, the burning fuse finally reached its target and the two sticks of dynamite ignited and exploded.

The explosion was huge and, consequently, the massive iron door of the safe was blasted wide open.

The outlaws slowly rose from behind the counter and surveyed the scene before them. A curtain of smoke filled the small office and then, as it dissipated, they were able to see into the safe. They had anticipated the shelves being filled with stacks of banknotes and bags of coins. Instead, to their shock and dismay, the outlaws observed that the shelves were completely empty.

'What in blue blazes!' exclaimed an irate Blair Wilton. 'Where in tarnation's the goddam money?'

'Gone,' said Gil Ambrose sombrely.

This statement of the obvious did not go down too well with the outlaw chief. He glared venomously at Ambrose and snarled, 'I can see that for myself. The point is, where's it gone?'

Ambrose and the Pearson cousins all shrugged their shoulders. Then, before any of them could reply, they were startled by the sound of a couple of shots, both of which emanated from outside.

'Oh, my God! Let's git the hell outa here!' cried Gil Ambrose.

'Yeah, let's!' echoed Frank and Hank Pearson in unison.

Blair Wilton said nothing, but immediately led the retreat from the bank. He and the others hastily grabbed up their saddle-bags, from where they had previously dropped them, and tumbled out of the back door.

Moments earlier, the sound of the explosion had awakened Chuck Finn. The young deputy had sprung to his feet and, drawing his Colt Peacemaker from its holster, rushed out of the law office into Main Street. Finding the street to be deserted, he had then run back into the office and exited through its rear door. At once, he had spotted the outlaws' horses grouped together behind the bank. And, in that same instant, Deadeye Drummond had shot him. Two slugs, one in the chest and one in the belly, had knocked him flat on his back.

Now, as the five outlaws swiftly mounted their horses, Chuck Finn lay in the dust, his life's blood slowly ebbing away.

'OK, boys, let's lam outa here!' yelled Blair Wilton.

The others needed no urging. They galloped after their leader, across the plain and away from the town, heading for the distant mountains.

Meanwhile, the explosion had abruptly interrupted Medicine Bow's church service. The pastor, who had been addressing his flock, had stopped in mid-sentence and several of the congregation had leapt to their feet. Jack Stone, who was sitting next to the aisle, in a pew near the back of the church, had straightaway risen and dashed towards the door. As he threw it open, the sound of Deadeye Drummond's gunshots echoed along the street.

'What can you see, Jack?' cried Vince Clayton.

'Not a goddam thing,' replied the Kentuckian, and he set off running down Main Street. He was closely followed by Clayton and several others, including the marshal, the mayor and his deputy and the manager of the Cattlemen's Bank.

As Stone and the others reached the vicinity of the bank, Seth Burroughs stepped out from the doorway

97

of the hotel opposite and accosted them. He rarely attended church, since he was not a particularly religious man.

'That explosion came from the bank an' the shots came from behind it,' he declared excitedly.

'You sure, Seth?' asked Sidney Greenridge.

'Certain.'

'OK. Hamilton, you got the keys?'

'I have,' replied the bank manager.

'Then, I suggest you open up.'

Hamilton Scott nodded and, producing a set of keys from his coat pocket, selected one and inserted it into the lock. He turned the key and pushed open the front door. Thereupon, he and the others tumbled into the bank.

There were gasps of surprise at the sight of the safe standing open and empty. Hamilton Scott was one of a number who simply stood and stared dumbfounded at the ransacked safe. Jack Stone and Marshal Joe Paine, meantime, hurried on through the bank and out through its rear door. Immediately, they spotted the bloodstained figure of Chuck Finn sprawled in the dirt behind the adjacent law office. Then, turning their heads, they observed Blair Wilton and his gang fast disappearing across the plain.

'Goddam those thievin', murderin' bastards!' exclaimed Joe Paine.

'Amen to that,' growled Stone.

'We gotta git after them,' rasped Paine.

'Any idea who they are, Marshal?' enquired the Kentuckian.

'I cain't be sure, but my guess is the Wilton gang. They recently tried robbin' a bank jest over the state line in Colorado.'

'Successfully?'

'Nope. This time, though, it seems they've cleaned up.'

'Yeah.'

'You aimin' to form a posse, Joe?' demanded Sidney Greenridge.

'I sure am,' said Paine. 'I wanta git the no-account critter who gunned down poor Chuck.'

'Me, too!' cried his other deputy, Ted Hume.

'I am sure we all do,' said Greenridge and, turning to Morris Broadfoot the town mortician, he remarked, 'You take care of Chuck's remains, Morris, while me an' some of the others git after his killers.'

'You volunteerin' to join the posse, Mr Mayor?' asked Paine, a little surprised.

'Of course. I feel it's my civic duty to do so,' retorted Greenridge piously.

Richard Thomas smiled. There were to be elections in November. This fact and the strong likelihood that the posse would fail to catch up with the outlaws were, he concluded, what had prompted

99

the mayor to offer to ride after them.

Several others also volunteered to be part of Marshal Joe Paine's posse. They quickly dispersed in order to saddle and mount their horses. Among those whose mounts were tethered outside the church was Jack Stone. He and Vince Clayton hurried off along Main Street in that direction.

'I'm afraid I cain't ride with you, Jack,' said Clayton as they strode out, half running and half walking.

' 'Course not. You ain't got no hoss,' replied the Kentuckian.

'No. Apart from the pair between the shafts of my buckboard. I could take one of them I s'pose, but I don't fancy ridin' bareback.'

'Don't worry, Vince. There are plenty of other folk in the same situation.'

This was true. Most of those from out of town, the ranchers and the homesteaders, had driven their families to church either on a buckboard or in a gig. Only one or two, like Stone, had ridden in on horseback.

On arrival at the church, Stone quickly mounted his bay gelding, while the rancher explained what had happened to his wife and children.

'Good luck, Jack!' cried Clayton. 'I hope you catch those thievin' murderers.'

'I'll sure do my best,' said Stone.

He turned the gelding's head and set off, back along Main Street, towards the bank. By the time he reached it, there were several others mounted and ready to ride.

Marshal Joe Paine sat astride a mettlesome black stallion. He reviewed his troops and addressed them thus: 'OK, boys, those varmints have got one helluva lead, so, without more ado, let's be after 'em. Prepare to ride like the wind!'

He set off through the town, quickly emerging on to the plain beyond. By now the outlaws were almost out of sight among the foothills of the Medicine Bow Range. Nevertheless, undeterred, the marshal and his posse galloped hell-for-leather after them.

At the same time that the posse left town, Blair Wilton pulled up his horse and raising his hand, brought the rest of the gang to a halt.

'Hell, Blair, what are we stoppin' for? I thought the plan was to ride straight on through the mountains to Providence Flats!' cried Deadeye Drummond.

'It was,' said Wilton,' but that was 'fore we hit town an' found someone else'd emptied the bank safe.'

'An' now?'

'We head back to the huntin' lodge. We got some thinkin' to do.'

'We could do that in Providence Flats.'

'Sure we could, Deadeye, but I wanta remain within' strikin' distance of Medicine Bow. At least for the time bein'.'

'OK. Then, shall we ride on?' asked Gil Ambrose, nervously eyeing the plain behind them.

'Yeah. There's soon gonna be a posse headin' this way,' added Hank Pearson.

'That's right,' said Wilton. 'Therefore, I figure it's best we split up an' make our separate ways to the huntin' lodge. We don't wanta leave tracks that can be easily followed.' He glanced round at each outlaw in turn. 'You all OK 'bout findin' your way there?' he asked.

'Yup,' said Deadeye Drummond, while the Pearson cousins merely nodded their heads.

'You, Gil?'

Gil Ambrose wasn't too sure, but didn't want to admit it.

'I guess so,' he mumbled.

'Right! See you boys at the lodge.'

So saying, Blair Wilton dug his heels into his horse's flanks and galloped straight ahead, up a narrow gulch that wound its way through the foothills towards the mountains beyond. His four confederates fanned out, each taking a separate route into the mountains.

Their pursuers, meanwhile, followed the outlaws' all-too-obvious tracks across the plain. The posse consisted of a dozen men, with Marshal Joe Paine and the Kentuckian, at their head and a nervous Sidney

Greenridge bringing up the rear on his ancient mare, Betsy.

In due course, the posse reached the spot where the Wilton gang had halted and, at their leader's behest, split up. They, too, halted while the marshal and Stone dismounted, crouched down and examined the tracks left by the outlaws. Their examination completed, the two men stood up and exchanged glances.

'Wa'al, what's the matter?' demanded Greenridge.

'It would seem the varmints have split up an' gone their separate ways. Ain't that so, Jack?' said Paine.

'Yup.'

'So, what do we do now?' asked the mayor.

'I guess we turn round an' head back to town.'

'But, Marshal—'

'Followin' single tracks through that there wild mountain terrain would be darned near impossible,' declared Paine.

'I agree,' said Stone, 'though I'm prepared to try an' follow one set of 'em.'

'You think you can, Jack?'

'I learned my trackin' skills from a Kiowa brave. So, I figure it's worth makin' the effort.'

'Then, lead on, Mr Stone. We'll follow,' said Greenridge.

'I'll be a sight quicker if I ride alone,' replied Stone. 'If 'n I catch up with the no-account critter I'll bring him in, never fear.'

'But s'pose he an' his accomplices are aimin' to meet up later at some hideout or other?' enquired the mayor.

'Then I'll report back as to where they're hidin' out.'

'But—'

'Jack's right. We'll only delay him,' growled Paine. He turned to face the Kentuckian and said, ' 'Bye, Jack. An' good luck!'

They watched as the Kentuckian galloped off. Unbeknown to him, Lady Luck was indeed smiling upon him, for he had chosen to follow the tracks of the least competent of Blair Wilton's riders, the Easterner Gil Ambrose.

'We could, I s'pose, follow one of them other sets of tracks,' suggested Ted Hume.

Joe Paine smiled wryly at his deputy.

'No,' he said. 'Jack Stone was once an army scout. I guess he jest might succeed in trackin' that single set. But I surely ain't got that kinda skill. Have any of you fellers?'

His deputy, and the mayor, and the rest of the posse reluctantly shook their heads.

'OK,' said the marshal. 'For us, the chase is over.'

And, accordingly, the posse turned round and headed back towards Medicine Bow.

# SEVEN

Since leaving the rest of the posse, Jack Stone had ridden no further than a couple of miles when he came upon his quarry. Gil Ambrose was an inexperienced rider and his lack of skill as a horseman had proved to be his undoing. He had attempted to clear a fallen tree, which was blocking the narrow gulch through which he was travelling, but his steed had clipped one of its branches, lost its stride and balance and fallen heavily. The grey gelding had then rolled over on top of its unfortunate rider and, upon staggering to its feet, had inadvertently trampled Ambrose and, in addition, dealt him a hefty blow to the chest. The horse had remarkably survived the fall without injury. However, the same could not be said of Gil Ambrose. His injuries were internal and fatal. When Stone reached him, he was near to death.

The Kentuckian swiftly dismounted and, drawing

his Frontier Model Colt, clambered over the fallen tree and crouched down beside the Easterner.

'OK,' he snarled,' your game's up.'

'I . . . I know . . . it . . . is. I'm done for,' croaked Ambrose.

Stone ran an eye over the outlaw. He nodded grimly. It was clear to him that Ambrose was dying. He slipped the revolver back into its holster.

'You one of the Wilton gang?' he growled, wanting to be sure that Marshal Joe Paine had guessed correctly.

Gil Ambrose saw no reason to deny it. He smiled weakly and murmured, 'Yeah, I . . . regret . . . to . . . say.'

'Wa'al, your accomplices won't be. Hell, they cleaned out that bank good an'—'

'No . . . they . . . didn't,' gasped Ambrose.

'Whaddya mean, no they didn't?'

'The safe was empty.'

'I don't understand.'

'When we . . . blew the safe open . . . we found it . . . was empty.'

'But—'

Stone cut short his question, for the other's head had suddenly fallen back and he was staring sightlessly up into the sky. The Kentuckian was completely bemused. What Gil Ambrose had just told him didn't make sense. It was frankly incredible. And yet why should the outlaw lie? What would be the point? Surely, with his dying breath, he would be bound to tell the truth?

Stone rose to his feet and walked across to where the grey gelding stood munching at a clump of tabosa grass. He opened each saddle-bag in turn. Both were empty. If the Wilton gang had taken the banknotes from the bank's safe, why were there none in these two saddlebags? Stone scratched his head. It sure was a mystery.

He went over to the fallen tree and, grabbing one end of it, heaved it sideways so that there was enough room for him to lead the grey gelding round to the other side. Then he draped Gil Ambrose's dead body across its saddle and secured it with some whipcord, which he had in his saddlebag. This done, he guided the gelding through the gap he had just made and, mounting his own horse, proceeded to lead the other by its bridle, back in the direction from which he had come.

It was still early afternoon when Jack Stone eventually rode into Medicine Bow. His arrival, together with the corpse of Gil Ambrose, created a minor sensation. A crowd quickly gathered outside the law office, where Stone had stopped and dismounted. As the Kentuckian tied his horse to the hitching rail, Marshal Joe Paine emerged from his office.

'So, you got one of the varmints, Jack!' cried Paine.

'Yeah.'

'Pity you had to shoot him. Otherwise, we could've—'

'I didn't shoot him.'

'No?'

'Nope. There was a fallen tree blockin' the trail. I figure he tried to clear it an' his horse fell an' rolled on him. He was pretty near to dyin' when I caught up with him.'

'I see. Were you able to question him 'fore he pegged out?'

'I was.'

'So?'

'So, let's call a council of war in your office.'

'That's right. Richard an' I wanta hear what you've gotta say,' said Sidney Greenridge.

'And me,' interjected Hamilton Scott, who, like the mayor and his deputy, had pushed his way to the front of the crowd.

'Fair enough,' said the marshal. He scanned the crowd for a sight of the town's mortician and, spotting him somewhere near the back, shouted, 'Mr Broadfoot, come through an' take care of this here dead body. Me an' the mayor, we'll head across to your funeral parlour an' settle matters with you jest as soon as we've finished talkin' to Jack.'

Morris Broadfoot, a tall, thin, lugubrious-looking man in a long black coat and tall stovepipe hat, slowly wended his way through the crowd. Then he took hold of the grey gelding's reins and led the horse and its lifeless rider off towards the funeral parlour.

While some of the crowd chose to follow Broadfoot, the vast majority remained outside the law office, anxious to discover what action would emanate from the council of war within.

Marshal Joe Paine ushered the others inside and quickly found chairs for the mayor, the deputy mayor and the bank manager. He himself sat in his usual chair behind his desk. Jack Stone indicated that he preferred to stand and Paine's surviving deputy, Ted Hume, had no option but to do the same. Thus was the council of war convened.

'OK, Jack,' said Paine, 'you said you were able to question that feller 'fore he died. So, tell us, what did you ask an' what did he have to say?'

'I asked him if he was one of the Wilton gang. He owned up that he was.'

'So, I guessed right. It was those no-account critters we saw ridin' off.'

'It sure was, Joe.'

'Did you ask him where his accomplices were headin' for?' demanded Greenridge.

'No, I didn't git the chance.'

'Did you ask him anythin' else?'

'No, Mr Mayor, I didn't. But, jest 'fore he breathed his last, he volunteered some information.'

'Indeed?' Richard Thomas peered eagerly at the Kentuckian.

'Yup. He told me that, when they blew open the safe, he an' his pardners found it to be empty.'

'Empty?' exclaimed Joe Paine.

'That's what the man said.'

'But ... but that's impossible,' stammered Greenridge.

'Unless. . . .' Thomas paused and then turned and stared accusingly at Hamilton Scott.

The bank manager blanched.

'You surely don't think that I emptied it? Why, in Heaven's name, would I do such a thing?' he expostulated.

'I don't know. But, if you didn't, who did?'

'If it was in fact empty. You have only the word of that outlaw to rely on,' said Scott.

'Why would he lie?' growled Stone.

'To protect his accomplices, perhaps?'

'In what way? Even if they didn't git the money, they still broke into the bank an' gunned down young Chuck Finn,' remarked Greenridge.

'That's right. There was no point in his lyin',' said Paine.

'I certainly b'lieved him,' declared Stone.

'Then, how the safe was emptied is a complete mystery,' said Scott. 'I swear to God it was stacked full of banknotes and coins when I locked up at five o'clock on Saturday evening. Indeed, my tellers will back me up.'

'You could have gone back later an' emptied it,' pointed out the marshal.

'You are welcome to search my house.'

'I don't think that'll be necessary, Mr Scott,' said Stone.

'You don't?' said Hamilton Scott.

'No. I've been thinkin' 'bout it ever since that feller told me the safe was empty.'

'You got a theory, Jack?' inquired Paine.

'Mebbe. What I wanta know is, have there been any strangers in town who have recently skedaddled?'

'Wa'al, there's Mr Jones from Chicago Premier Real Estate Inc. You met him in the saloon 'bout noon on Friday,' said Greenridge.

'An' there was that feller sellin' his so-called miracle medicine out of a covered wagon. Doc Harris, I seem to recall he called hisself,' said Paine.

'Them two fellers knew each other,' remarked Ted Hume.

Marshal Paine looked hard at his deputy.

'How'd you know that, Ted?' he asked.

' 'Cause I heard Mr Jones address the other feller as Fingus.'

'Fingus? But, accordin' to the legend printed on the side of his wagon, he was named Dr Septimus Harris.'

'Wa'al, that's what I heard Mr Jones call him.'

'Fingus?'

'Yeah, Marshal. Ain't that an Irish name?'

'Supposin' you heard it correctly,' said Stone.

'I'm sure I did,' declared the deputy.

'Could it have been Fingers rather than Fingus?'

Hume thought about this for a moment or two.

'I guess it could,' he said finally.

'So, what if it was?' Paine, enquired of the Kentuckian.

'Fingers is the kinda nickname sometimes given to a safe-breaker, a cracksman,' replied Stone. 'Wa'al, assumin' that there dyin' outlaw was tellin' the truth, it would have taken a top-notch cracksman to break open the safe an' then close it again after removin' its contents. I'm guessin' Mr Jones an' Fingers, or Doc Harris, or whatever his real name is, were workin' together.'

'Are you sayin' that they entered an' robbed the bank last night an' then, by sheer coincidence, Blair Wilton an' his gang raided it the followin' mornin'?'

'No, Marshal, I ain't sayin' that,' said Stone.

'Then, what in tamation are you sayin'?'

'I b'lieve Mr Jones was sent into town by Blair Wilton, in order to reconnoitre it before he an' his men rode in an' raided the bank. Then, quite by chance, he spotted Doc Harris, who happened to be an old acquaintance of his from Chicago.'

'Hmm. I s'pose that's possible,' mused the marshal. 'I heard a feller, by the name of Allan Pinkerton, is busy cleanin' up that city an', in consequence, several of its less reputable citizens have fled.'

'So, you're sayin' that Paul Jones wasn't a representative of Chicago Premier Real Estate Inc., that he was some kinda criminal?' cried Sidney Greenridge.

'That's my guess,' said Stone.

'An' I reckon Jack's right,' added Paine.

'But . . . but I . ., that is, we. . . .' mumbled the mayor, glancing unhappily at the bank manager.

'Gave the sonofabitch a guided tour of the bank,' Hamilton Scott finished Greenridge's sentence for him.

'Yes. He . . . he was so convincing!'

'We were all taken in, Sidney,' said his deputy, patting the mayor sympathetically upon the shoulder.

'If . . . if Jack *is* right.'

'I'm sure he is,' stated Paine. 'I reckon, when Jones spotted Doc "Fingers" Harris, he got the idea of double-crossin' Blair Wilton. That way the loot would be split two ways instead of six. That's your theory, ain't it, Jack?'

'Yup.'

'But when did Paul Jones an' Doc Harris leave town, that's the question?' said Richard Thomas.

'It has to be sometime durin' the early hours of

this mornin',' replied Paine.

'I agree,' said Stone.

'The dirty, schemin', thievin' varmints!' exclaimed Greenridge. 'Hell, if that dyin' desperado hadn't spilled the beans to Mr Stone, we'd still be thinkin' it was Blair Wilton an' his gang who had robbed the bank!'

'We all agree with you there, Sidney,' said Thomas. 'But what now? Jones an' Harris have one heck of a start on us an' we don't know in which direction they are headin'.'

'Wa'al, the main trail through here runs east to west,' said Stone.

'An' if, as seems likely, they're travellin' in Harris's wagon, then they ain't gonna be movin' very fast,' remarked Paine.

'They could have split up,' suggested Deputy Hume glumly.

'I don't think so. That feller Jones struck me as bein' a pretty shrewd character. I reckon he'll expect Blair Wilton to put two an' two together an' finger him as a double-crosser. But, as far as he's aware, Wilton knows nuthin' of Doc Harris an' his part in the affair. Therefore, Wilton an' his boys will be out lookin' for a single horseman, not for a coupla fellers ridin' a wagon. Leastways, I figure that's what Jones will assume. What do you think, Jack?'

'I b'lieve you're right, Marshal.'

'So, whaddya gonna do?' enquired the mayor anxiously.

'If Jack's prepared for me to swear him in as a deppity,' said Paine, 'I propose we both hit the trail, one of us headin' east an' the other west. A wagon will need to stick to the main trail, an', providin' we ride hard an' fast, I figure one or other of us should catch up with it 'fore the day is out.'

'Hey, what about me?' cried Hume.

'You'll be needed here in town. With Chuck Finn dead an' me off in pursuit of them two miscreants, you're the only remainin' law officer. You'll be actin' marshal in my absence,' said Paine.

'Will I?' ejaculated the elderly Hume, smiling delightedly at the prospect.

'Indeed you will, Ted.' Paine turned to the Kentuckian. 'Wa'al, whaddya say, Jack?' he asked.

'OK, Joe. Swear me in. Only someone will need to let Vince know that it could be a li'l while 'fore I return to the ranch.'

'I'll ride over an' tell him,' volunteered Sidney Greenridge. 'I was intendin' to speak to him anyway 'bout purchasin' me a hoss to replace ole Betsy.'

The others nodded. Betsy had served the mayor for more years than enough. She deserved to be put out to grass.

'Right,' said Paine to Stone, 'raise your right hand.'

It took only a few moments for the Kentuckian to be sworn in as a deputy. Then he and the marshal quickly discussed which direction each should take. It was decided that he should head west while Joe Paine headed east. Minutes later, they set out.

Jack Stone rode hard and fast. The afternoon was wearing on and he wanted to catch up with Doc Harris's wagon before nightfall. Whether or not that was possible, he wasn't sure.

A brief stop at the way-station, where unbeknown to him Paul Springer had rendezvoused with Blair Wilton, confirmed that he was in fact heading in the right direction. The proprietor, Panama Pete, had that morning observed the wagon bearing the legend, *Dr Septimus Harris's Miracle Cure for All Ails*, on its side. The wagon was, he stated, travelling westward and it had two men up on the box. Jack Stone thanked the half-breed and resumed his ride. He galloped off in the direction of Walcott, the next town along the trail.

## EIGHT

At about the same time that Jack Stone was entering Medicine Bow, towing Gil Ambrose's corpse, Blair Wilton was riding up to the hunting lodge from which he and his gang had set forth that very morning.

A piebald was hitched to the rail outside the lodge. Blair Wilton smiled. He recognized the animal as the steed of Deadeye Drummond. As he approached, the lodge's door was flung open and the small, squint-eyed, weaselly outlaw stepped out onto the stoop.

'Hi, Blair!' he cried. 'You made it then.'

'Yup.'

'So, what now?'

'We wait for the others.'

In the event, the Pearson cousins turned up a quarter of an hour later. Then, while they waited for Gil Ambrose, the outlaws brewed some coffee and fetched out a few strips of beef jerky. And, as they voraciously consumed these victuals, they discussed the mystery of the empty safe.

'Empty! The darned safe was completely empty! How in blue blazes could that be?' demanded Deadeye Drummond irately.

'It don't make no sense,' declared Hank Pearson.

'It sure don't,' confirmed his cousin.

An atmosphere of gloom prevailed as the four desperadoes sat mulling over in their minds the details of their failed bank raid. Everything had gone according to plan, Paul Springer's plan. They had entered the bank unobserved and blown open the safe. Inside should have been a large quantity of banknotes and coins. Yet, in the event, the safe had contained precisely nothing.

Blair Wilton eventually broke the silence.

'There's only one feasible explanation,' he growled.

'Oh, yeah? An' what's that, Blair?' inquired Drummond.

'That we was betrayed.' Wilton paused and then added bitterly, 'By that skunk, Paul Springer.'

'What are yuh sayin', that Springer spilt the beans to the marshal an' that the marshal arranged for the money to be removed?'

'No, Deadeye, that ain't what I'm sayin'.'

'Then I don't understand.'

'If 'n Springer had informed the marshal of our plans, an ambush would surely have been set for us? But it wasn't.'

'That's true. The marshal an' the rest of the townsfolk didn't come a-runnin' till they was alerted by us blowin' the safe.'

'An' you figure that means they knew nuthin' about our proposed robbery?' said Frank Pearson.

'Correct.' Blair Wilton scowled. 'Springer emptied the goddam safe. I'm certain of it,' he rasped.

'But how?' enquired a mystified Hank Pearson.

'Wa'al, he sure as hell didn't blow the safe!' exclaimed Frank Pearson.

'A top-notch safe-breaker could've cracked the combination an' then reset it,' suggested Drummond.

'Exactly,' said Wilton.

'But . . . but Paul Springer wasn't no top-notch safe-breaker,' protested Hank Pearson.

'We don't know that,' said Drummond.

'If he had've been, why didn't he say so? Why persuade Blair to buy them sticks of dynamite?'

'Mebbe, Hank, he was aimin' to double-cross us from the start,' said Wilton. 'I mean, it was his idea for us to wait till Sunday mornin' 'fore ridin' into town.'

'Yeah.'

'By which time he planned to have cleaned out the safe an' be long gone, leavin' us to take the blame.'

'That certainly seems to be the most likely explanation for what's happened,' said Drummond. 'The only other one I can think of, is that someone else chose last night to rob the bank.'

'In which case, Paul Springer will be headin' for Providence Flats, where he's expectin' to meet up with us an' git his share of the loot,' said Hank Pearson.

'Hmm. Someone else choosin' to rob the bank only a few hours 'fore we did is too much of a coincidence. I jest don't buy it,' said Wilton. 'No; Springer double-crossed us an' made off with the contents of that safe.'

The others slowly nodded their heads. Then Deadeye Drummond spoke up.

'OK,' he said. 'Let's assume Blair's right. So, what are we waitin' for?'

'Gil Ambrose,' said Frank Pearson. 'Where in tarnation has he got to?'

'I figure he's got plumb lost,' opined Blair Wilton.

'Or been taken by that posse we spotted settin' out after us,' remarked Drummond.

'More likely he's lost, for my guess is that the posse turned back once they realized we'd split up.'

'Yet, if 'n he has been taken, he could mebbe lead the posse to this here huntin' lodge,' said Frank Pearson.

'That's true. Therefore, hadn't we best lam outa

here?' enquired his cousin anxiously.

'We had,' growled Wilton. 'But not jest for that reason. We gotta catch up with Springer an' git our hands on all that loot he took from the bank.'

'But, Blair, he's got one helluva start on us, an' we ain't got a clue which direction he took,' commented Drummond.

'We'll ride back down through the mountains towards Medicine Bow,' said Wilton.

'But if there's a posse out lookin' for us. . . .' began Drummond.

'Then, they sure as hell won't be expectin' us to head in that direction.'

'Even so, I don't reckon. . . .'

'There's a way-station a few miles outa Medicine Bow. I wanta call in there,' said Wilton. He offered no explanation, but simply made for the door. He flung it open and, beckoning the others to follow him, rasped, 'We mount up an' go. Now!'

The outlaws hurried out of the hunting lodge, clattered across the stoop and down the short flight of wooden steps to the ground. They swiftly unhitched and mounted their horses and, with Blair Wilton leading, set off down through the mountains towards the plain and the trail below. The rough, rugged terrain prevented them from riding at full gallop, as they made their descent through both black brush and forest.

Presently, however, they emerged onto the plain and, upon reaching the trail, rode hell-for-leather along it until the way-station came into view. Half a mile short of it, there was a small stand of timber. It was in front of this that Blair Wilton brought the cavalcade to a halt.

'OK, boys, hide yourselves among those trees while I visit the way-station,' he commanded.

'Why are you goin' there?' asked Deadeye Drummond curiously.

'I'm hopin', with a bit of luck, to pick up some news 'bout our friend, Paul Springer,' replied Wilton.

'Really?'

'It's a long shot. But, like you said earlier, we don't know in which direction he's headin'. An', if we're gonna catch him, that's somethin' we need to know.'

'Yeah, that's fact. Wa'al, good luck!'

The Pearson cousins echoed Deadeye Drummond's words and then followed him into the trees.

Meanwhile, Blair Wilton rode slowly up to the way-station. Since there were no horses hitched to the rail outside, he guessed there were no travellers inside. He dismounted and entered the building. He had guessed correctly. The general store-cum-bar-room was deserted except for the short, fat figure of Panama Pete presiding behind his large wooden counter. A glint of recognition sparked in the half-breed's eyes and his mouth split into an enormous grin.

'Ah, *señor*, you are back so soon!' he greeted the outlaw.

'An' why shouldn't I be?' retorted Wilton.

'No reason, *señor*. It is just that most of my customers are merely passing through and, so, I never see them again. You, however, I saw yesterday and now—'

'I'm back again,' Wilton finished the half-breed's sentence for him.

'*Sí, señor.*'

'I'm a travellin' man,' said Wilton.

'Ah, so it is possible I may see you again?'

'That's right.'

'Well, how may I help you?'

'I fancy a beer. I got me one helluva thirst.'

'*Sí*, it is hot out on the trail.'

'Sure is.' Wilton smiled at his host. 'Will you join me?' he asked.

'*Muchas gracias, señor.*'

'You're pretty quiet this afternoon,' commented Wilton, while the other poured the two beers.

'We were busy enough this morning.'

'Oh, yeah?'

'*Sí, señor*. Many travellers. More than usual for the Sabbath.' Panama Pete paused and then continued,

'Some men from Medicine Bow brought disturbing news. Their bank had been robbed. They said that the marshal led a posse off in pursuit of the robbers.'

'Did they mention who the robbers were?'

'They were not sure, but thought it was the Wilton gang.'

'Indeed?'

'*Sí.*' Panama Pete raised his glass. 'To the capture of those accursed desperadoes!' he cried.

Blair Wilton also raised his glass, but did not repeat the half-breed's toast. Both men drank thirstily.

'Do you recall the feller I was with yesterday?' enquired Wilton, as he lowered his glass.

'I do, *señor.*'

'We was s'posed to meet some ways down the trail. But he failed to turn up. Don't expect you've seen him today?'

Panama Pete smiled widely.

'*Sí,*' he said.

'You have? When?'

'Early this morning. It is my custom to rise early, in order to feed the chickens, pick up the eggs and milk the goat before my customers arrive. I was returning from doing these chores when I observed a covered wagon approaching from the direction of Medicine Bow. As it passed by, I noticed that one of the two men on the box was your friend.'

'You don't say!'

'But I do, *señor*. I am certain it was he.'

'This wagon. Can you describe it?'

Blair Wilton asked this question more in hope than in expectation, for one covered wagon looks much like another. Consequently, Panama Pete's reply came as a welcome surprise.

'The wagon had words printed on its side.' Panama Pete puffed out his chest. 'I have a good memory. I remember the words exactly,' he declared proudly.

'Then, spit 'em out!' rasped Wilton.

'*Sí, señor*. The words were: *Dr Septimus Harris's Miracle Cure for All Ails.*'

An evil grin split Blair Wilton's ugly features. He finished his beer in one draught, slapped the empty glass down onto the counter and tossed a handful of coins across it towards the half-breed.

'Here, have another drink on me,' he growled.

'And one for yourself?'

'No, I'm outa here.'

'You intend to pursue your friend?'

'Yup.'

'Is Dr Septimus Harris also a friend of yours?'

'Er . . . no, he's not. Why d'you ask?'

'Only because, *señor*, somebody else asked me whether the doctor had passed by in his wagon.'

'Somebody else? Who?'

'I do not know. A big man on a bay gelding.'

'A lawman?'

'Perhaps, though I do not think he was wearing a badge.'

Blair Wilton scowled. Even though the big man on the bay gelding had not been displaying a badge, the outlaw felt sure he must be a peace officer, presumably despatched from Medicine Bow to hunt down Paul Springer and the mysterious purveyor of medicine. Why else would he have been enquiring about them? That they had emptied the bank's safe, Wilton was convinced. And also that they had intended him and his gang to take the rap. However, if the big man was, as he supposed, a peace officer, then somehow or other Springer's ploy had failed. There was no time to lose. He needed to catch up with Dr Harris and his erstwhile accomplice before the law did.

'Jest when did the big feller ask about the doctor an' his wagon?' he demanded.

'About half an hour ago,' replied Panama Pete.

'Thanks.'

Blair Wilton turned and strode briskly out of the way-station. He quickly mounted his horse and set off westward along the trail, towards the stand of timber where he had left his confederates. As he reached it, Deadeye Drummond and the Pearson cousins rode out from among the trees.

'Wa'al, whaddya find out?' asked Deadeye Drummond eagerly.

'Our quarry are headin' west. They passed the way-station early this mornin',' said Wilton.

'They?'

'It seems Paul Springer has a pardner.'

'Who, for Pete's sake?'

'Some goddam quack, name of Dr Septimus Harris.' Wilton grimaced and asked, 'Whaddya wanta hear first, the good news or the bad news?'

'The good news,' said Hank Pearson.

'They're travellin' by wagon.'

'Which means pretty darned slowly,' said Frank Pearson, grinning.

'Yup. With luck, we could overtake 'em sometime this evenin'.'

'So, what's the bad news?' enquired Deadeye Drummond.

'There's a lawman hot on their trail an' he has half an hour's start on us.'

'Holy cow!' exclaimed Drummond.

'So, boys, we ain't got a moment to lose. Let's git ridin'!' cried Wilton.

So saying, he dug his heels into his horse's flanks and set off at a gallop. The rest of the gang sped after him. Their steeds' hoofs pounded the bone-dry earth, creating in their wake a cloud of dust, as they were ridden at breakneck speed, westward after their quarry.

# NINE

Keith Muldoon, nicknamed Fingers and alias Dr Septimus (or Doc) Harris, was feeling very pleased with himself as he drove the wagon towards the small cowtown of Bitter Creek. It was mid-morning and he and his companion, Paul Springer, had, since leaving Medicine Bow that morning, passed through no fewer than four townships: Walcott, Sinclair, Rawlins and Creston. Their failure to stop at any of them had gone unremarked in all bar Rawlins, where a number of its citizens had demanded to know why the good doctor wasn't proposing to pause and sell his *Miracle Cure for All Ails*. Muldoon had explained that, so popular had it been, his supplies were completely sold out. He was, he had assured them, on his way to pick up some more.

'I'll be back,' he had lied cheerfully.

Safely stowed away in the back of the wagon,

beside those bottles of the famous *Miracle Cure*, which he did in fact still possess, were the contents of the safe he had cracked open back in Medicine Bow. The combination lock had proved difficult to pick, but not impossible for a safe-breaker of Muldoon's skill and dexterity. The wizardry, which had made him a key member of Big Tony Demarco's Chicago gang, had stood him in good stead.

He glanced at his companion. Their unexpected encounter had been extremely fortuitous. Back in Chicago he would have barely acknowledged the other man, for, while he was one of Big Tony's lieutenants, Paul Springer had been nothing more than a small-time gambler, card sharp, gigilo and confidence trickster. This fact had made him rather reluctant to listen to Springer's proposition. He was glad, however, that he had relented and paid attention to what the other had to say.

Muldoon smiled inwardly. Paul Springer's plan had been simple. The two of them would break into the Cattlemen's Bank in the small hours of Sunday morning, Muldoon would crack the safe's combination lock, they would gather up its contents, then Muldoon would reset the locks of both the safe and the bank's rear door. Consequently, when Blair Wilton and his gang raided the bank as arranged, later that same morning, they would blow open an empty safe, but still take the blame for the robbery.

That had been Springer's simple yet brilliant plan, and it had worked perfectly. Muldoon laughed out loud.

'What's ticklin' you?' enquired Paul Springer curiously.

'I was jest thinkin' 'bout the look on Blair Wilton's face when they blew open that safe an' found nuthin' inside. It must've been a picture,' he chuckled.

Springer joined in the laughter.

'It sure must,' he agreed. 'My li'l ploy puts us in the clear. Nobody's gonna be out lookin' for us. The word will be out that the Wilton gang has robbed another bank.'

'That's so.'

' 'Course, if one or other of 'em should git caught. . . .'

'He'll claim the safe was empty.'

'But nobody will believe him, Fingers.'

'No.' Muldoon smiled and, changing the subject slightly, asked, 'If you hadn't spotted me in Medicine Bow, would you have gone through with your original pact with Blair Wilton?'

'Of course.'

'So, why the double-cross? Surely—'

'This way I git half the loot. If I'd stuck with Blair an' the boys, I'd've got only one-sixth.'

'Yeah, that makes sense.'

'Also, I figured a safe-breaker of your reputation

would be almost certain to crack open that safe. I wasn't so sure that Blair would succeed in blowin' it. He wasn't no expert when it came to handlin' dynamite.'

'Ah!'

'An', since you an' me would be raidin' the bank in the middle of the night, there was little likelihood of the forces of law an' order descendin' upon us.'

'Whereas, once Blair Wilton blew the safe open, all hell would be let loose.'

'That's right, Fingers.'

'Smart thinkin', Paul.'

'You said, when first we met, that your ambition was to open a saloon, or a dance-hall, or a gamblin' joint in 'Frisco. Wa'al, now you can.'

'Yup.' Muldoon smiled at his companion and asked, 'An' what about you?'

Springer returned the other's smile and shrugged his shoulders.

'I dunno,' he said. 'I ain't got no hard 'n' fast plans. Reckon, to start with, I'll jest have me a good time.'

'Whereabouts you got in mind?'

'Wa'al, we're headin' in the general direction of 'Frisco. Like you, I may decide to settle there. Mebbe we could go into business together?'

'Mebbe.'

'Our first venture went well.'

'Couldn't have gone better.'

'Wa'al, then?'

Fingers Muldoon hesitated. He had certain reservations and he needed a little time to reflect upon them before saying either yes or no. He continued to smile.

'You said you were intent on jest havin' a good time,' he said.

'To start with. We could both begin by enjoyin' what 'Frisco has to offer an' then, when we've sampled sufficient of its pleasures, meet an' set up a joint business venture. Whaddya say?'

Muldoon continued to both smile and hesitate.

Finally, he said, 'Let's not be hasty. We've got several hundred miles to cover 'fore we reach 'Frisco. I'll think about it.'

'Sure. Take your time.'

Springer couldn't understand why the other should vacillate. Yet he appreciated that there was no immediate need for Muldoon to come to a decision. He had plenty of time, and, anyway, Springer was convinced he would in due course accept his, Springer's proposal.

However, in making this assumption, Paul Springer was wrong.

As he drove the wagon along the trail towards Bitter Creek, the white-haired, benevolent-looking purveyor of medicine was harbouring thoughts which were anything but benevolent. In his long black coat and battered stovepipe hat, he might look like some rather shabby, out-of-work undertaker, benign and to all intents and purposes harmless, but he was nothing of the kind.

Keith 'Fingers' Muldoon was giving his present situation a great deal of consideration. Both he and Springer naturally believed that Blair Wilton and his associates were currently being pursued by the forces of law and order for the robbery of the Cattlemen's Bank in Medicine Bow, and that, consequently, he and Springer were in the clear. However, that didn't mean they were altogether out of danger. Muldoon feared danger might come from a different quarter.

'Blair Wilton ain't no fool,' he said.

'No, I'll grant you that,' replied Springer.

'I assume that most likely, in the aftermath of him an' his gang blowin' that safe, a posse would've been got up to pursue 'em.'

'I guess so.'

'It could've caught up with 'em.'

'Yup.'

'But let's suppose it didn't, that he an' his men escaped into the mountains.'

'Yeah, that's quite probable. I mean, their raid was scheduled to coincide with the church service. By the time the townsfolk—'

'Quite so,' Muldoon cut the other short and then

went on, 'Once he was sure they'd shaken off their pursuers, Blair Wilton would have had time to think. An' whaddya s'pose he'd have been thinkin' about?'

' 'Bout the raid.'

'An' the fact that the safe was empty.'

' 'Course.'

'So, what's he gonna make of that?'

'Like you said, Blair ain't no fool. He's gonna come to the conclusion that I double-crossed him an' am responsible for emptyin' the safe. Mind you, he'll wonder how I managed it. Mebbe he'll assume that I was, after all, a skilled cracksman, yet chose to keep this a secret from him.'

'Or that you had a confederate.'

'Yes.'

'But he won't know who that confederate is.'

'No.'

'Either way, it's you he'll be lookin' for.'

'Exactly.' Springer grinned. 'Should he an' his gang happen along this way, we'll be sure to hear the thunder of their hosses' hoofs long before they catch up with us. This'll give me plenty of time to clamber into the back of the wagon, where I can hide till they've gone past. Blair certainly won't be on the outlook for *Dr Septimus Harris* an' his *Miracle Cure for All Ails.*'

Muldoon smiled complacently since he was unaware that both Blair Wilton and the law, in the person of Jack Stone, had in fact discovered that he and Paul Springer were in cahoots, and were in hot pursuit. For the present, he felt safe from the outlaw chief's vengeance. It was the future that troubled him. It was not impossible that sometime, weeks, months, or even years from now, Wilton would turn up in 'Frisco. And if he did. . . .

Muldoon could not afford to take the risk that Wilton might discover Springer there. Should he do so, Wilton would want to know how Springer had succeeded in cracking that safe. And Muldoon did not trust Springer to keep his mouth shut. The one-time confidence trickster would squeal, of that Muldoon was certain. And then Wilton would come after him. Well, he told himself, that could not be allowed to happen.

As these thoughts crossed his mind, Muldoon spied, no more than a mile away, the small township of Bitter Creek. It was by now quite dark and light spilled out on to Main Street from the windows and doors of houses, shops, stores and saloons. Up above was a bright starlit sky and over the tops of the town's other buildings could be seen the tall, narrow spire of its one and only church pointing towards the heavens. Muldoon stared hard and long at this spire, all the while continuing to reflect upon his situation. Finally, he determined upon what he must do.

' 'Bout us goin' into partnership together,' he said.

'Yeah?' responded Springer eagerly.

'I've been thinkin' an' I guess we could do worse.'

'So, all we gotta do now, is decide what kinda business we wanta buy into?'

'That's correct.'

As he spoke, Muldoon tugged on the reins and gradually brought the horses and the wagon to a standstill.

'Hey, what are you doin'?' enquired Springer.

'I thought I'd halt the wagon so as we can turn an' face each other, an' shake hands on the deal.'

'Oh, right!'

The two men swivelled round on the box until they were face to face. Immediately, Muldoon extended his right hand towards his companion. And, in that same instant, a short, squat, double-barrelled derringer suddenly appeared from inside the sleeve of his coat. It was pointed straight at Springer's heart.

' 'Bye, Paul. It's been nice knowin' you,' said Muldoon drily.

The Chicago confidence trickster's jaw dropped and, belatedly, he attempted to pull his .30 calibre long-barrelled Colt from its shoulder rig. But his hand had barely closed round the butt before the first of Muldoon's shots struck him in the chest. A second quickly followed and Springer fell backwards off the box, down onto the trail.

he and Springer had passed that day. Then there was always a chance that the finder of the body would recognize Springer as one of the two men he had earlier seen riding the wagon bearing the legend: *Dr Septimus Harris's Miracle Cure for All Ails.* The chance was slight, yet Muldoon was not prepared to risk it.

He had another plan. The sight of the church spire had given him the idea. It was now late Sunday evening. There would be no more church services that day. Indeed, there was unlikely to be another until the following Sunday. Therefore, should he conceal Paul Springer's body inside the church, a week would most probably elapse before it was discovered. And, by then, he would be over a hundred miles away and within a few days' ride of 'Frisco, where he intended abandoning the wagon and assuming yet another pseudonym. He grinned. It was a simple plan, but one which he was convinced would prove foolproof.

Late Sunday evening in Bitter Creek found its streets pretty much deserted. Muldoon drove the wagon across the town limits and down Main Street. During his progress along this thoroughfare he observed fewer than a dozen people. Four cowboys spilled out of one of its saloons and proceeded to mount up, preparatory to heading back to their ranch. Two couples crossed the street and entered its only hotel, and three of the town's storekeepers stood outside their separate premises, smoking and enjoying the cool evening air. None seemed to be the slightest interested in his passage through the town.

At the far end of Main Street were a few dwelling houses and, last of all, the small wooden church with its spire and, directly opposite, what Muldoon took to be the pastor's house. He noted that both the church and the pastor's house lay in darkness. The pastor was surely, he reckoned, a man who abided by the old adage: *Early to bed, early to rise, makes a man healthy, wealthy and wise.*

A wicked grin split Muldoon's bewhiskered features as he brought the wagon to a halt immediately in front of the church. He dismounted and glanced back along Main Street. Of the people he had passed, only one of the storekeepers was still visible, and that was because he remained standing in the light spilling out of his front doorway. The others were swallowed up by the darkness. Muldoon concluded, therefore, that, if he could not see them, then they could not see him and his wagon.

He hurried towards the church and tried the door handle. Had the door been locked, he was ready to use his expertise to break in. However, this proved to be unnecessary. The handle turned and he found he was able to push the door inwards. He stepped inside.

Muldoon stood for a moment or two to allow his eyes to become accustomed to the gloom. Light from the starlit sky filtered through the church's windows and was sufficient for him to survey its interior. On either side of the central aisle rows of pews stretched down towards the pulpit, the chancel and, ultimately, the altar. Muldoon smiled. He would dump Paul Springer's body in one of the two rear-most pews, as far away from the central aisle as possible. Then, providing his premise that there would be no weekday services proved true, the corpse should lie there undetected until the following Sunday. Even should the pastor pop in and out of the church in the meantime, it was unlikely he would spot Springer's body at the far end of the pew.

Muldoon promptly turned on his heel and headed back towards the wagon. He climbed up into the rear of it and pitched Springer's corpse out. Then he dropped down beside the dead man and proceeded to drag him by his heels towards, and into, the church. Once inside, Muldoon heaved the body along the left-hand rear-most pew to its far end, where he let go of it. Thereupon, wiping his perspiring brow, he turned again and made his way back along the pew to the central aisle. As he stepped into the aisle, his heart missed a beat. A dark figure stood silhouetted in the doorway, confronting him.

The Reverend Martin Smith was twenty-six years old and Bitter Creek was his first parish. Of medium height and slim built, the pastor had a youthful countenance and was good-looking, though perhaps not conventionally handsome, with his snub nose and wide mouth. A pair of twinkling blue eyes completed the picture.

He had been visiting a young widow who ran a dry goods store in the town. Her husband had died of a fever three years earlier and, as a regular churchgoer, she had been among the first to greet the pastor on his arrival. During the twelve months since the Reverend Smith had taken up his ministry, he and the widow had become fast friends. Their friendship had blossomed and that very evening he had proposed to her and been accepted. Consequently, he was in a state that could only be described as euphoric, as he strode home following their happy and eventful supper together.

He was approximately one hundred yards away, when he observed the wagon standing in front of the church. Then, to his surprise and consternation, he saw Fingers Muldoon drag Paul Springer's body out of the wagon and across the few yards separating it from the house of God. As Muldoon vanished inside, the Reverend Martin Smith broke into a run.

Now he stood in the doorway and confronted the confidence trickster's murderer.

'What, in the name of God, do you think you are doing?' he demanded angrily.

Muldoon quickly recovered his composure. The sudden appearance of the young clergyman had given him a shock, but he was nothing if not resourceful. Noting that his challenger was alone, he smiled grimly and drew the derringer from inside the sleeve of his coat. He pointed it at the young man.

'What business is it of yours?' he snarled.

'This is the church of which I am the appointed minister,' replied the Reverend Smith.

'Oh, really?'

'Yes. And I want to know what devilment you are up to? Was that a dead body you dragged in here?'

'You had best see for yourself,' said Muldoon. He gestured with the derringer that the pastor should proceed into the church. Then, stepping aside, he ushered the young man into the pew, at the end of which he had dumped the late, unlamented Paul Springer. His plan was straightforward. He would shoot the pastor and leave his corpse, together with Springer's, to be discovered, he hoped, no earlier than the following Sunday. Facing his intended victim, he said quietly, 'I'm a reasonable man, Reverend. So, I'm gonna give you time to say a li'l prayer before I shoot you.'

'This is the house of God,' protested the Reverend Smith. 'What you are proposing is not only murder. It is sacrilege!'

Muldoon laughed harshly.

'Spare me that religious rubbish,' he snapped. 'I

ain't no—'

But he never completed the sentence, for while he had been conversing with the young pastor, a third figure had entered the church and crept up behind him. The newcomer had then pulled a revolver from its holster, reversed it and, with all the force he could muster, clubbed Muldoon on the back of the skull. The killer pitched forward to sprawl senseless across the aisle.

'Wow! That was a close thing,' gasped the Reverend Smith. 'I surely thought I was going to die.'

'Yeah, guess I arrived in the nick of time,' said the other.

'I am in your debt, Mr . . . er. . . ?'

'Stone. Jack Stone. An' you are. . . ?'

'The Reverend Martin Smith. This is my church and, when I saw this feller drag what looked like a dead body inside, I came to investigate. Can you tell me, what on earth is going on here?'

'In the early hours of this mornin' the Cattlemen's Bank in Medicine Bow was robbed by the man who threatened you an' his accomplice.' Stone stepped into the rear-most pew and, finding Paul Springer's body on the floor at its far end, growled, 'His late accomplice. Guess either they fell out or this one' – here he prodded the unconscious Muldoon with the toe of his boot – 'got greedy.'

'An' jest where do you come into all of this?'

143

enquired the clergyman.

'I was appointed deppity by the marshal back at Medicine Bow. I've been ridin' hell-for-leather after these two varmints since early this afternoon.'

'But if the robbery took place in the early hours of the morning. . . .'

'I'd better explain,' said Stone.

He proceeded to tell the pastor of all that had taken place that morning and how he had learned from Gil Ambrose that the safe at the Cattlemen's Bank had been empty when the Wilton gang blew it open. He went on to explain how he and the others had figured out that the pair known as Paul Jones and Doc Harris had stolen the money and, in so doing, double-crossed Blair Wilton and his gang.

'Gee, that's some story, Mr Stone!' exclaimed the young pastor. 'So, where do you think all that money is now? In that wagon outside?'

'That's my guess,' said Stone.

'Then let's go look.'

'One moment, Reverend.'

Stone stepped towards the doorway and cautiously peered outside. His keen hearing had picked up the thunder of horses' hoofs. Now he saw them, the dark shapes of four fast-approaching horsemen. He watched as they drew up beside the wagon and dismounted.

'What . . . what are we waitin' for?' asked the

Reverend Smith.

'Those four fellers who've ridden up. I reckon they're what's left of the Wilton gang,' said Stone in a low voice.

'No!'

'I'm 'fraid so. Seems Blair Wilton figured things out, too. Only I got here first.'

'So, what do you propose, Mr Stone?'

'Wa'al, I sure as hell ain't gonna let 'em grab that money an' vamoose.'

'But you cain't hope to out-shoot all four of 'em.'

'I can try.'

'No, Mr Stone. Let me join you an' together. . . .'

The Kentuckian smiled warmly at the young clergyman.

'You're a man of the cloth, not a gunslinger,' he said. 'An' this ain't your fight, Reverend. Therefore, do me a favour an' stay inside this here church until the shootin's over.'

'But—'

'I 'preciate your offer, but I cain't accept it.'

So saying, Jack Stone turned abruptly and stepped out through the open doorway and into the night.

The Reverend Martin Smith opened his mouth to protest, then changed his mind and, instead, made his way swiftly down the aisle towards the chancel. A door to the left of the chancel afforded access to his vestry. He thrust this open and disappeared inside.

# TEN

Blair Wilton and his gang had ridden like the wind to catch up with Paul Springer and Keith 'Fingers' Muldoon. As a result, they had ridden into Bitter Creek only a few minutes after their quarry and the pursuing Kentuckian had hit town.

Like Jack Stone before him, Blair Wilton had observed the wagon outside the church and had read the legend printed on its canvas side. Smiling triumphantly, he had brought his small cavalcade to a halt and signalled that they should dismount.

Drawing his Colt Peacemaker, Wilton cautiously approached the wagon. He noted that the box was unoccupied and he drew back the canvas flap at its rear and peered inside.

'Hmm,' he muttered. 'Seems there ain't nobody at home. No Springer an' no Dr Septimus Harris.'

'So, where in tarnation are they?' demanded

Deadeye Drummond.

'How the hell should I know?' growled Wilton. 'Anyways, let's give the wagon the once-over.'

'You bet,' said an eager Hank Pearson and, seconds later, both he and his cousin had clambered aboard.

There was a single kerosene lamp hanging from the roof of the wagon. Frank Pearson quickly produced a box of lucifers and proceeded to light the lamp. The resulting illumination showed the wagon to contain a few cooking utensils, some blankets and a couple of straw mattresses, and several large medicine chests.

'Wa'al, what have we got here?' rasped Wilton, as he and Drummond climbed in beside the two cousins.

'Them medicine chests . . .' began Frank Pearson.

'Open 'em,' commanded Wilton.

When their lids were thrown back, the first three revealed nothing other than bottles of Dr Septimus Harris's famous medicine. The fourth, however, proved to be full to the brim with banknotes of various denominations. This discovery brought forth whoops of delight from Frank and Hank Pearson.

'Keep the noise down,' hissed Wilton. 'Darn it, you'll wake up the whole goddam town!'

'That's right. An' you wouldn't wanta do that, would you?' came a voice from outside.

The four outlaws hastily tumbled out of the back of the wagon and found themselves face to face with the Kentuckian. A distance of no more than twenty feet separated the outlaws and the lawman.

'Who in blue blazes. . . ?' began Blair Wilton.

'Jack Stone's the name,' replied the Kentuckian. 'An' you must be the notorious Blair Wilton.'

The outlaw chief swallowed hard. He had heard of Stone. Who hadn't? The man was a living legend of the West, the last man on earth Wilton wanted to tangle with. Yet, if it came to a gunfight, the odds were four to one in his, Wilton's, favour. Even so, maybe it need not come to that. Wilton determined to negotiate.

'Whaddya want, Mr Stone?' he asked quietly.

'To take you an' your gang in, an' hand you over to the marshal here in Bitter Creek,' replied Stone.

'On what charge?'

'Charges. Robbery an' murder.'

'Aw, come now, you don't really wanta do that!'

'No?'

'Hell, no! You know what's lyin' inside that there wagon?'

'The proceeds of this mornin's raid on the Cattlemen's Bank in Medicine Bow.'

'You got it, Mr Stone.'

'So?'

'We didn't take that money.'

'I realize that, but you did raid the bank an' gun down Deppity Marshal Chuck Finn.'

Blair Wilton shrugged his shoulders.

'The deppity tried to prevent us escapin'.'

'An' paid for it with his life.'

'Sure. But you needn't do the same. Should you try to arrest us, you most surely will. You cain't hope to out-shoot all four of us.'

'You reckon?'

'I know you're fast. You got one helluva reputation. But me an' the boys, we're also pretty darned quick with a gun. We have a shoot-out, you're dead for certain, an' one or mebbe two of us. Now that ain't sensible. So, let's make a deal.'

'A deal?'

'Yup. In the absence of Paul Springer an' his pal, we was aimin' to split their takin's four ways. Whaddya say, Mr Stone? Will you settle for one fifth of what we found in the wagon?'

'Hell, Blair, I don't think—' began Deadeye Drummond in protest.

'Shuddup, Deadeye. This way we're all winners. You wanta end up a corpse?' rasped Wilton.

The squint-eyed, weasely little outlaw looked less than happy to share, yet his chief's final few words had sent a shiver down his spine.

'Guess not,' he muttered.

'So?'

'OK, we do it your way, Blair.'

Wilton turned to the two Pearson cousins.

'An' you two? You both in agreement with this?'

Neither spoke, but simply nodded their heads.

Blair Wilton smiled wryly and turned to face the Kentuckian.

'There you are, Mr Stone,' he said. 'Me an' the boys are prepared to offer you a fifth share, providin' you jest ride off an' forget you ever saw us. Now ain't that handsome of us?'

'Not handsome enough,' said Stone.

'You want more?' exclaimed Wilton.

Stone shook his head.

'Nope. I ain't buyin',' he replied.

'But—'

'You mentioned my reputation, part of which is, I ain't never yet succumbed to a bribe.'

'Mebbe nobody's ever offered you one till now?'

'Mebbe. Mebbe not.'

'Then. . . ?'

Stone shook his head a second time.

'No deal,' he said.

Wilton scowled. He desperately wished to avoid a gunfight, for, while he was pretty certain that Stone would not survive, he was also pretty certain that the Kentuckian would take down at least a couple of the outlaws with him. And he had a nasty feeling that he would be the first to be targeted.

'Aw, come on!' he remonstrated. 'You cain't hope to beat the odds. They're four to one against you.'

'Four to two.'

Stone turned to find the Reverend Martin Smith standing beside him. The young pastor smiled and calmly pushed back his long black coat to reveal a pair of matched pearl-handled forty-five calibre British Tranters, one on each thigh.

Stone glanced down at the two hand-guns in amazement.

'Where in tarnation did you git them, Reverend?' he gasped.

'I'll tell you later,' whispered the young minister. 'For now, how do we play this?'

Stone reverted his gaze to the four desperadoes facing him. Starting from his right, they lined up as follows: Firstly Blair Wilton, then Deadeye Drummond, next Frank Pearson, and on Stone's extreme left Hank Pearson.

'I'll take the two on the right,' he replied out of the corner of his mouth.

'OK,' said the Reverend Smith.

Realizing that further negotiation was useless, Wilton finally lost patience and yelled, 'Doggone it, I've had enough of this!'

And he went for his gun.

The gunfight was brief but bloody. Both Stone and the pastor dropped into a crouch as they drew and fired their revolvers.

Stone's first shot struck Blair Wilton in the chest and knocked him backwards a good six feet, while Wilton's shot, a split second after the Kentuckian's, passed harmlessly over Stone's head. Deadeye Drummond, meantime, loosed off a couple of quick shots. Unfortunately for him, neither found its target. Speed had taken precedence over accuracy and, in consequence, one bullet whistled past Stone's left ear while the other ripped through the fabric of his buckskin jacket, grazing his left arm as it flew by. Stone's response was deadly. His second slug hit the outlaw between the eyes and blasted his brains out of the back of his skull.

Neither of the Pearson cousins was particularly quick on the draw, whereas the Reverend Martin Smith matched the Kentuckian for both speed and accuracy. Hank Pearson's Colt Peacemaker was only halfway out of its holster when the pastor's first shot slammed into his chest. The pastor's second went straight through Frank Pearson's neck, demolishing his Adam's apple in the process. With a fountain of blood spurting forth from the wound in his throat, the desperado staggered forward a few paces, then fell face downwards into the dust, his half-raised gun slipping from his nerveless fingers.

A profound silence followed, during which the Kentuckian carefully examined the fallen outlaws.

Blair Wilton, Deadeye Drummond and Hank Pearson were dead. Only in Frank Pearson was there still a spark of life. But his life's blood was oozing away and, a few moments later, he, too, breathed his last.

Jack Stone regarded the pastor with a quizzical eye.

'This ain't the first time you've shot a man,' he commented.

'No,' said the Reverend Smith, pulling his coat about him so as to hide the two British Tranters, which he had dropped back into their holsters.

Stone replaced the Frontier Model Colt in its holster and asked, 'You gonna explain?'

'Sure thing, Mr Stone,' replied the other. 'But can it wait till after we've spoken to the marshal?'

He pointed down Main Street at two men who were hurrying towards them, evidently anxious to investigate the shooting which had so abruptly disturbed the peace and quiet of that August evening.

'OK,' said Stone.

'And, can you do me a favour? Will you claim credit for the deaths of all four of the Wilton gang?'

The Kentuckian stared in surprise at the young man.

'But—'

'Please, Mr Stone.'

Stone recalled the sight of the pair of matched

pearl-handled forty-five calibre British Tranters now hidden beneath the pastor's coat. When and where had such a pair featured in recent years? Not too many shootists favoured two guns. And not too many chose a British Tranter as their hand-gun. However, five or six years earlier. . . . Stone smiled as he suddenly remembered.

'OK, Reverend,' he said. 'We'll play it your way.'

'Thank you.'

They turned to watch Bitter Creek's marshal and his deputy approach. Both were short of breath upon arrival, for they were in their late fifties and rather corpulent.

'Jeeze!' Then spotting the Reverend Smith, the marshal apologized, 'Sorry, Reverend, but what in . . . er . . . what's been goin' on? I mean, all these corpses. Who. . . ?'

'The four dead men are Blair Wilton an' three of his gang,' explained Stone. 'They were involved in a bank robbery back in Medicine Bow. I was deputized to go after 'em. Jack Stone's the name, by the way.'

'Gee, Mr Stone, it's sure a pleasure to meet you, sir! You got one helluva reputation,' stated the marshal. 'Bill Cameron at your service, an' this here's my deppity, Stan Peters.'

'Howdy.'

'Yeah . . . howdy.' Marshal Cameron stared awestruck at the four bodies. 'You out-drew an' out-shot all four of 'em?' he gasped.

'He certainly did,' interjected the Reverend Smith.

'Holy cow!' exclaimed the marshal.

'That must've been somethin' to behold!' added his deputy.

'Yeah, wa'al, let me tell you the whole story,' said Stone.

He then proceeded to repeat everything he had earlier told the pastor, and finished by recounting how Keith 'Fingers' Muldoon had murdered his accomplice and had been surprised by the Reverend Smith as he attempted to hide his victim inside the church.

'Fortunately, Mr Stone turned up when he did, otherwise I'd've suffered the same fate,' remarked the pastor. 'He KO'd the ruffian.'

'Wa'al, I'll be doggoned!' cried Bill Cameron. Then, turning to his deputy, he said, 'You'd best git into the church an' slap some cuffs on that feller 'fore he comes to.'

'Sure thing, Marshal.'

While Deputy Peters was thus occupied, the marshal climbed into the wagon and took a long, hard look at the medicine chest full of banknotes. He scratched his head.

'Looks like I'm gonna be kinda busy,' he mused.

'You are indeed, Marshal,' said Stone. 'I suggest

you drive the wagon into town an' place those bank-notes somewhere safe. In your local bank, mebbe? Then, you can wire your opposite number in Medicine Bow an' make arrangements to transfer the money back to where it belongs, in the Cattlemen's Bank from which it was stolen.'

'Good thinkin', Mr Stone. That's exactly what I'll do.'

At this moment, Deputy Peters emerged from the church, escorting a handcuffed and extremely groggy Fingers Muldoon. It would be some time before the murderer recovered from the hefty blow dealt him by Jack Stone.

'What'll I do with him now?' enquired Peters.

'Jest march him into town an' stick him in a cell,' replied the marshal. He glared at Muldoon and rasped, 'That feller you shot may be a no-account bank robber, but you'll still hang for his murder. You can depend on that!'

Muldoon scowled, but said nothing as he was led away by the deputy. Marshal Bill Cameron watched them head on into town and then climbed through the back of the wagon, on to the box.

'You comin', Mr Stone?' he asked.

The Kentuckian shook his head.

'Not yet, Marshal. I'll join you presently. But, first, I'm gonna give the Reverend a hand to carry that dead man outa the church. We'll leave him here beside the other corpses.'

'Yes. Perhaps you will ask Mr Potter to come and collect all five, and take them to his funeral parlour,' said the young pastor. 'Although they are robbers and murderers, nevertheless they are entitled to a Christian burial.'

'Yessir,' said Bill Cameron, although with little enthusiasm and little conviction.

While the marshal turned the wagon round and set off in the wake of Stan Peters and his prisoner, Jack Stone and the Reverend Martin Smith returned to the church and, together, carried the corpse of Paul Springer outside. They dumped his body between those of Blair Wilton and Deadeye Drummond.

'Now,' said Stone, 'we got some talkin' to do.'

'Yes. I have a confession to make.'

'Your surname ain't Smith. It's Sawyer.'

'Ah, you've guessed!'

'It suddenly came to me. 'Bout five, six years back a young gunslinger made quite a name for hisself in the Lincoln County range war. Then, all at once, he disappeared an' ain't been heard of since. He was last seen in Rifle, a small town in Colorado. His name was Kid Sawyer an' he was famous for totin' a pair of pearl-handled British Tranters.'

'That was me,' said the pastor. 'However, my surname is in fact Smith. I had it changed by deed poll.'

157

'Oh, yeah?'

'Yes. I felt the need for a clean break. When I was run outa town by Rifle's sheriff, I was hurting badly. If I'd ridden out onto the plains, I'd've died for sure. But, unbeknown to the sheriff and the rest of Rifle's citizens, I fell off my horse and was taken in and cared for by the local minister and his wife. The minister persuaded the doctor, who happened to live next door, to tend to my wound and keep his mouth shut. Between them they saved my life.'

'You were lucky.'

'I was. Mighty lucky, for that experience changed my thinking and my whole way of life. I found God, or perhaps I should say, He found me.' The late Kid Sawyer and present Reverend Smith smiled beatifically and went on, 'As a hired gun, I'd accumulated a fair amount of money. I used this to put myself through a theological college in Boston. I passed the course with honours and was subsequently ordained. This is my first parish.'

'Wa'al, congratulations, Reverend,' said Stone, 'for it's all too easy to take the wrong path. It ain't so easy, though, to git off it an' back on to the straight an' narrow. That takes true grit.'

'I trust my secret is safe with you?'

' 'Course it is, Reverend.'

'Thank you.'

'Jest one thing, though. Why did you hold onto

them British Tranters?'

'I dunno. I never meant to use them again. I guess, because they'd served me well, I didn't want to part with them. So, I kept them hidden at the back of a cupboard in my vestry.'

'It was as well for me that you did.'

'I s'pose so.'

'For a man who ain't fired a gun in five, six years, you did pretty darned good.'

'I like to think I had the Lord on my side.'

'Wa'al, He sure wasn't likely to be on the side of Blair Wilton an' his bunch of desperadoes,' chuckled Stone.

'No,' said the pastor. 'I don't expect He was.'

As he spoke, the Reverend Martin Smith unstrapped his gun-belt and passed it and the two holstered revolvers to the Kentuckian.

'What's the idea?' asked Stone.

'Take them, sell them, do what you like with them. I think it's now time I gave them up. This has been my last shoot-out.'

'OK, I'll stick 'em in one of my saddlebags an' sell 'em when I git back to Medicine Bow. But, for now, I'd best go join the marshal an' see how he's gittin' on with his arrangements. You comin'?'

The Reverend Smith shook his head.

'Later, perhaps,' he said. 'Firstly, I must give thanks to God for our deliverance.'

'Ah, yes!' Stone smiled. 'Guess the marshal can wait a while. I'll join you, if I may?'

'You're most welcome,' replied the pastor.

He stretched an arm round Jack Stone's broad shoulders and the two men went back into the church.